W9-CTS-163

MASTER STORYTELLERS SERIES

THE BIRTHMARK
and other stories by
NATHANIEL HAWTHORNE

Edited, with an introduction, a biographical sketch, and a selective bibliography by

Maxine Greene
Teachers College
Columbia University

SBS SCHOLASTIC BOOK SERVICES
New York • London • Richmond Hill, Ontario

Special contents copyright © 1968 by Scholastic Magazines, Inc. This edition is published by Scholastic Book
Services, a division of Scholastic Magazines, Inc.

1st printing .... Spring 1968

Printed in the U.S.A.

 # CONTENTS

INTRODUCTION

WHEN YOU BEGIN reading these stories by Nathaniel Hawthorne, you will (if you permit yourself to do so) be entering a romantic, mysterious world. Try to *picture* what is happening as you read, and you will find yourself witnessing remarkable things. You will see dimly lit scenes set in forests where the sun breaks unevenly through the black pines and moonlight makes the hidden clearings seem alive with shadowy forms. You will see winding, lamplit village streets; cottages where people huddle by their firesides; a laboratory lit by the glow of a red-hot furnace; a witch's dusky kitchen; silvery puddles on gabled roofs. There will be faces suddenly illuminated by glancing lights. You may catch a glimpse of the Prince of Darkness, momentarily visible in the glimmer of the moon. A black-draped face will stare into a mirror and retreat in horror. A lovely woman's face, marred by a tiny mark in the shape of a hand, will hold you for an instant. You will confront a grotesque gentleman's face and wonder if it can really be red and black at once.

You will, in fact, see many reds and blacks in Hawthorne's imaginary world. You may begin to associate the reds with warmth, excitement, passion, companionship in the public world. The dark shades may make you think of loneliness, separateness, feelings of sinfulness, secret guilts. The colors will clash and sometimes merge with one another, as one character after another tries to come to terms with the strangeness of the universe and, at once, with the strangeness in himself.

Hawthorne, who was born in 1802, liked to write about America in its early days when the strain of living in a strange new world was deeply felt. Certainly, life was more dangerous two centuries ago than it was in Hawthorne's own time or than it is today. Many towns bordered on the wilderness, and the inhabitants could never feel entirely safe from Indian raids, witches' spells, or the other nameless dangers that seemed to lurk in the trackless woods. Nor could they feel sure of their own impulses — the wishes their ministers said were sinful, the desires for independence, the yearnings to be free.

And this may be what brings the stories close to you. You may find them presenting experiences that you recognize somehow, for all the distance between you and Goodman Brown, Aylmer, Reuben Bourne, and the boy named Robin, who is just eighteen years old. Have you not, at some time in your life, been tempted to leave the security of your home for the world outside — perhaps for the wilderness of the downtown streets? Have you not sometimes wondered how you could live up to the demands of the adults around you and at the same time be yourself? Have you not — perhaps once — been disappointed in some older person you admired? Have you not felt disillusioned by imperfection?

Ideas like these will not be spelled out in everyday language in the stories you are about to read. To come upon them, to discover what you secretly understand, you will have to let your imagination play. You will have to move quietly inside yourself and try to see with your own inner eye what Hawthorne has to show.

Fortunately, he was one of the greatest word painters who ever lived; and you will find it easy to visualize his forests, streets, windows, and shadowy, flickering rooms. It will not be unreasonable for you to imagine the scenes you are about to witness as if they were being shown on a television screen. Although Hawthorne was fascinated with mirrors, lenses, and the early cameras, he could not, of course, have anticipated television. Even so, he composed his stories pictorially, alternating close-ups with distance shots, composing each scene as if he were preparing it for filming. A view of a vast congregation of people fades into close-ups of the fitfully illuminated faces of a deacon, an old woman, a pale young wife. A view of a cluster of townsfolk in their Sunday best gives way to a

sharply focused picture of a black veil, which
is studied for a moment until the imaginary camera moves down to reveal the gentle mouth and
the chin. A picture of the great spaces of the
forest contracts until two wounded men are revealed, one of them clearly marked for death.
An image of a churning crowd on a Boston dock
becomes an image of an adolescent's eyes peering through the night.

This is all done by means of language, which
is used — as it always is in fiction — in a rather
special way. You would not be able to visualize
so much if Hawthorne were writing in the kind
of language used for newspaper articles and factual reports. That sort of language must be direct
and clear. The words selected must be words
that refer, quite simply, to specific objects and
events. There must be as little vagueness as possible. The words must not be ambiguous. This
means they must not be open to more than one
interpretation: they must not be equivocal.

The imaginative writer, like Hawthorne,
starts with the same raw material, the very language used for ordinary conversation and report-
ing. But he uses this material to *suggest* as often
as to say. He shapes it, plays with it in such a
way that very common terms function to arouse
all kinds of feelings in the reader, all sorts
of remembered experiences — yes, and pictures
too. How does he do this? By comparing things
that ordinarily would not be linked together:
someone's eyes, for example, are said to be "like
fire in a cave"; a minister's quiet joke affects
his listeners "like a cheerful gleam from a

hearth"; silk stockings on a scarecrow's legs are "as unsubstantial as a dream." When you read, then, about the look of a particular individual's eyes, you will find yourself thinking at the same moment of a fire in a cave; and the feelings such an image awakens in you will be attached to the look of those eyes. That is what will happen in the case of all such figures of speech, similes, or metaphors. And that is one reason why you will see so much if you attend to the life of the words.

Hawthorne also exploits ambiguities, uses them in all sorts of dramatic ways. This is not because he wants to confuse you. It is because he wants you to realize that many of the situations in life — and certainly the situations he presents — are open to more than one interpretation. One of the marvelous things about his stories is that they are susceptible to several kinds of interpretation. Perhaps what happens is a dream; perhaps it is not. Supernatural forces seem to have been at work; but it is possible to explain every remarkable incident in completely natural terms. You will be able to explain something as mere accident or coincidence; at the same time you will realize that it might have been preordained. This is the source of the mysteriousness hovering over every one of these stories. Everything that happens is made to seem ambiguous.

You will discover, therefore, that every story holds a kind of puzzle for you to solve: a peculiar human predicament, a problem intensely felt. You are going to encounter all sorts of people at moments of dramatic personal crisis. One critic has said that Hawthorne began each story by asking himself, "What would happen if . . . ?" And then he would deliberately place a character or a group of characters under stress in order to see what would happen and to enable others to see.

The plots are not neatly worked out the way mystery-story plots are. There are no predictable endings; sometimes there is no clear ending at all. This is because Hawthorne sees the world that way. He was interested in the mysterious aspects of human behavior, fascinated with half-tones, half-lights, and — again — ambiguities. As his reader, you will have the opportunity to make your own interpretations and discover your own meanings, since there *is* no single "correct" answer to any of the puzzlements here.

For each story in this book there is a brief informal note. These notes begin on p. 205 of the text and may be read before you read a story or afterward if you prefer. These notes are not intended to sum up the stories, to give you the answers, to tell you what the tales "really mean." They are intended to entice you into the imaginary world created by the story and to point to some of the sights you can see in that world if you attend to the language, if you allow yourself to become involved.

That, after all, is the important thing: to get caught up in each of these miraculous tales; to live for some moments in these created worlds; to enjoy what you feel and see. Happy voyaging — and try not to lose your way.

YOUNG GOODMAN BROWN

Young Goodman Brown came forth at sunset into the street at Salem village; but put his head back, after crossing the threshold, to exchange a parting kiss with his young wife. And Faith, as the wife was aptly named, thrust her own pretty head into the street, letting the wind play with the pink ribbons of her cap while she called to Goodman Brown.

"Dearest heart," whispered she, softly and rather sadly, when her lips were close to his ear, "prithee put off your journey until sunrise and sleep in your own bed tonight. A lone woman is troubled with such dreams and such thoughts that she's afeared of herself sometimes. Pray tarry with me this night, dear husband, of all nights in the year."

"My love and my Faith," replied young Goodman Brown, "of all nights in the year, this one night must I tarry away from thee. My journey, as thou callest it, forth and back again, must needs be done 'twixt now and sunrise. What, my sweet, pretty wife, dost thou doubt me already, and we but three months married?"

"Then God bless you!" said Faith, with the pink ribbons; "and may you find all well when you come back."

"Amen!" cried Goodman Brown. "Say thy prayers, dear Faith, and go to bed at dusk, and no harm will come to thee."

So they parted; and the young man pursued his way until, being about to turn the corner by the meetinghouse, he looked back and saw the head of Faith still peeping after him with a melancholy air, in spite of her pink ribbons.

"Poor little Faith!" thought he, for his heart smote him. "What a wretch am I to leave her on such an errand! She talks of dreams, too. Methought as she spoke there was trouble in her face, as if a dream had warned her what work is to be done tonight. But no, no; 'twould kill her to think it. Well, she's a blessed angel on earth; and after this one night I'll cling to her skirts and follow her to heaven."

With this excellent resolve for the future, Goodman Brown felt himself justified in making more haste on his present evil purpose. He had taken a dreary road, darkened by all the gloomiest trees of the forest, which barely stood aside to let the narrow path creep through, and closed immediately behind. It was

all as lonely as could be; and there is this peculiarity in such a solitude, that the traveler knows
not who may be concealed by the innumerable
trunks and the thick boughs overhead; so that
with lonely footsteps he may yet be passing
through an unseen multitude.

"There may be a devilish Indian behind every
tree," said Goodman Brown to himself; and he
glanced fearfully behind him as he added, "What
if the devil himself should be at my very elbow!"

His head being turned back, he passed a crook
of the road, and, looking forward again, beheld the figure of a man, in grave and decent attire, seated at the foot of an old tree. He arose at
Goodman Brown's approach and walked onward
side by side with him.

"You are late, Goodman Brown," said he.
"The clock of the Old South was striking as I
came through Boston, and that is full fifteen minutes agone."

"Faith kept me back a while," replied the
young man, with a tremor in his voice, caused
by the sudden appearance of his companion,
though not wholly unexpected.

It was now deep dusk in the forest, and deepest in that part of it where these two were journeying. As nearly as could be discerned, the
second traveler was about fifty years old, apparently in the same rank of life as Goodman
Brown, and bearing a considerable resemblance
to him, though perhaps more in expression than
features. Still they might have been taken for
father and son. And yet, though the elder per-

son was as simply clad as the younger, and as simple in manner too, he had an indescribable air of one who knew the world, and who would not have felt abashed at the governor's dinner table or in King William's court, were it possible that his affairs should call him thither. But the only thing about him that could be fixed upon as remarkable was his staff, which bore the likeness of a great black snake, so curiously wrought that it might almost be seen to twist and wriggle itself like a living serpent. This, of course, must have been an ocular deception, assisted by the uncertain light.

"Come, Goodman Brown," cried his fellow traveler, "this is a dull pace for the beginning of a journey. Take my staff, if you are so soon weary."

"Friend," said the other, exchanging his slow pace for a full stop, "having kept covenant by meeting thee here, it is my purpose now to return whence I came. I have scruples touching the matter thou wot'st of."

"Sayest thou so?" replied he of the serpent, smiling apart. "Let us walk on, nevertheless, reasoning as we go; and if I convince thee not thou shalt turn back. We are but a little way in the forest yet."

"Too far! too far!" exclaimed the Goodman, unconsciously resuming his walk. "My father never went into the woods on such an errand, nor his father before him. We have been a race of honest men and good Christians since the days of the martyrs; and shall I be the first of the name of Brown that ever took this path and kept — "

"Such company, thou wouldst say," observed the elder person, interpreting his pause. "Well said, Goodman Brown! I have been as well acquainted with your family as with ever a one among the Puritans; and that's no trifle to say. I helped your grandfather, the constable, when he lashed the Quaker woman so smartly through the streets of Salem; and it was I that brought your father a pitch-pine knot, kindled at my own hearth, to set fire to an Indian village, in King Philip's war. They were my good friends, both; and many a pleasant walk have we had along this path, and returned merrily after midnight. I would fain be friends with you for their sake."

"If it be as thou sayest," replied Goodman Brown, "I marvel they never spoke of these matters; or, verily, I marvel not, seeing that the least rumor of the sort would have driven them from New England. We are a people of prayer, and good works to boot, and abide no such wickedness."

"Wickedness or not," said the traveler with the twisted staff, "I have a very general acquaintance here in New England. The deacons of many a church have drunk the communion wine with me; the selectmen of divers towns make me their chairman; and a majority of the Great and General Court are firm supporters of my interest. The governor and I, too — But these are state secrets."

"Can this be so?" cried Goodman Brown, with

a stare of amazement at his undisturbed companion. "Howbeit, I have nothing to do with the governor and council; they have their own ways, and are no rule for a simple husbandman like me. But, were I to go on with thee, how should I meet the eye of that good old man, our minister, at Salem village? Oh, his voice would make me tremble both Sabbath day and lecture day."

Thus far the elder traveler had listened with due gravity; but now burst into a fit of irrepressible mirth, shaking himself so violently that his snakelike staff actually seemed to wriggle in sympathy.

"Ha! ha! ha!" shouted he again and again; then composing himself, "Well, go on, Goodman Brown, go on; but, prithee, don't kill me with laughing."

"Well, then, to end the matter at once," said Goodman Brown, considerably nettled, "there is my wife, Faith. It would break her dear little heart; and I'd rather break my own."

"Nay, if that be the case," answered the other, "e'en go thy ways, Goodman Brown. I would not for twenty old women like the one hobbling before us that Faith should come to any harm."

As he spoke he pointed his staff at a female figure on the path, in whom Goodman Brown recognized a very pious and exemplary dame, who had taught him his catechism in youth, and was still his moral and spiritual adviser, jointly with the minister and Deacon Gookin.

"A marvel, truly, that Goody Cloyse should be so far in the wilderness at nightfall," said he.

"But with your leave, friend, I shall take a cut through the woods until we have left this Christian woman behind. Being a stranger to you, she might ask whom I was consorting with and whither I was going."

"Be it so," said his fellow traveler. "Betake you to the woods, and let me keep the path."

Accordingly the young man turned aside, but took care to watch his companion, who advanced softly along the road until he had come within a staff's length of the old dame. She, meanwhile, was making the best of her way, with singular speed for so aged a woman, and mumbling some indistinct words — a prayer, doubtless — as she went. The traveler put forth his staff and touched her withered neck with what seemed the serpent's tail.

"The devil!" screamed the pious old lady.

"Then Goody Cloyse knows her old friend?" observed the traveler, confronting her and leaning on his writhing stick.

"Ah, forsooth, and is it your worship indeed?" cried the good dame. "Yea, truly is it, and in the very image of my old gossip, Goodman Brown, the grandfather of the silly fellow that now is. But — would your worship believe it? — my broomstick hath strangely disappeared, stolen, as I suspect, by that unhanged witch, Goody Cory, and that, too, when I was all anointed with the juice of smallage, and cinquefoil, and wolf's bane — "

"Mingled with fine wheat and the fat of a newborn babe," said the shape of old Goodman Brown.

"Ah, your worship knows the recipe," cried the old lady, cackling aloud. "So, as I was saying, being all ready for the meeting, and no horse to ride on, I made up my mind to foot it; for they tell me there is a nice young man to be taken into communion tonight. But now your good worship will lend me your arm, and we shall be there in a twinkling."

"That can hardly be," answered her friend. "I may not spare you my arm, Goody Cloyse; but here is my staff, if you will."

So saying, he threw it down at her feet, where, perhaps, it assumed life, being one of the rods which its owner had formerly lent to the Egyptian magi. Of this fact, however, Goodman Brown could not take cognizance. He had cast up his eyes in astonishment, and, looking down again, beheld neither Goody Cloyse nor the serpentine staff, but his fellow traveler alone, who waited for him as calmly as if nothing had happened.

"That old woman taught me my catechism," said the young man; and there was a world of meaning in this simple comment.

They continued to walk onward, while the elder traveler exhorted his companion to make good speed and persevere in the path, discoursing so aptly that his arguments seemed rather to spring up in the bosom of his auditor than to be suggested by himself. As they went, he plucked a branch of maple to serve for a walking stick, and began to strip it of the twigs and little boughs, which were wet with evening dew. The moment his fingers touched them they became strangely withered and dried up as with a week's sunshine. Thus the pair proceeded, at a good free pace, until suddenly, in a gloomy hollow of the road, Goodman Brown sat himself down on the stump of a tree and refused to go any farther.

"Friend," said he, stubbornly, "my mind is made up. Not another step will I budge on this errand. What if a wretched old woman do choose to go to the devil when I thought she was going to heaven: is that any reason why I should quit my dear Faith and go after her?"

"You will think better of this by and by," said his acquaintance, composedly. "Sit here and rest yourself a while; and when you feel like moving again, there is my staff to help you along."

Without more words, he threw his companion the maple stick, and was as speedily out of sight as if he had vanished into the deepening gloom. The young man sat a few moments by the roadside, applauding himself greatly, and thinking with how clear a conscience he should meet the minister in his morning walk, nor shrink from the eye of good old Deacon Gookin. And what calm sleep would be his that very night, which was to have been spent so wickedly but so purely and sweetly now, in the arms of Faith! Amidst these pleasant and praiseworthy meditations Goodman Brown heard the tramp of horses along the road, and deemed it advisable to conceal himself within the verge of the forest, conscious of the guilty purpose that had brought him thither, though now so happily turned from it.

On came the hoof tramps and the voices of the riders, two grave old voices, conversing soberly as they drew near. These mingled sounds appeared to pass along the road, within a few yards of the young man's hiding place; but, owing doubtless to the depth of the gloom at that particular spot, neither the travelers nor their steeds were visible. Though their figures brushed the small boughs by the wayside, it could not be seen that they intercepted, even for a moment, the faint gleam from the strip of bright sky athwart which they must have passed. Goodman Brown alternately crouched and stood on tiptoe, pulling aside the branches and thrusting forth his head as far as he durst without discerning so much as a shadow. It vexed him the more, because he could have sworn, were such a thing possible, that he recognized the voices of the minister and Deacon Gookin, jogging along quietly, as they were wont to do, when bound to some ordination or ecclesiastical council. While yet within hearing, one of the riders stopped to pluck a switch.

"Of the two, reverend sir," said the voice like the deacon's, "I had rather miss an ordination dinner than tonight's meeting. They tell me that some of our community are to be here from Falmouth and beyond, and others from Connecticut and Rhode Island, besides several of the Indian powwows, who, after their fashion, know almost as much deviltry as the best of us. Moreover, there is a goodly young woman to be taken into communion."

"Mighty well, Deacon Gookin!" replied the

solemn old tones of the minister. "Spur up, or we shall be late. Nothing can be done, you know, until I get on the ground."

The hoofs clattered again; and the voices, talking so strangely in the empty air, passed on through the forest, where no church had ever been gathered or solitary Christian prayed. Whither, then, could these holy men be journeying so deep into the heathen wilderness? Young Goodman Brown caught hold of a tree for support, being ready to sink down on the ground, faint and overburdened with the heavy sickness of his heart. He looked up to the sky, doubting whether there really was a heaven above him. Yet there was the blue arch, and the stars brightening in it.

"With heaven above and Faith below, I will yet stand firm against the devil!" cried Goodman Brown.

While he still gazed upward into the deep arch of the firmament and had lifted his hands to pray, a cloud, though no wind was stirring, hurried across the zenith and hid the brightening stars. The blue sky was still visible, except directly overhead, where this black mass of cloud was sweeping swiftly northward. Aloft in the air, as if from the depths of the cloud, came a confused and doubtful sound of voices. Once the listener fancied that he could distinguish the accents of townspeople of his own, men and women, both pious and ungodly, many of whom he had met at the communion table, and had seen others rioting at the tavern. The next moment, so indistinct were the sounds, he doubted whether he had heard aught but the murmur of the old forest, whispering without a wind. Then came a stronger swell of those familiar tones, heard daily in the sunshine at Salem village, but never until now from a cloud of night. There was one voice of a young woman, uttering lamentations, yet with an uncertain sorrow, and entreating for some favor, which, perhaps, it would grieve her to obtain; and all the unseen multitude, both saints and sinners, seemed to encourage her onward.

"Faith!" shouted Goodman Brown, in a voice of agony and desperation; and the echoes of the forest mocked him, crying, "Faith! Faith!" as if bewildered wretches were seeking her all through the wilderness.

The cry of grief, rage, and terror was yet piercing the night, when the unhappy husband held his breath for a response. There was a scream, drowned immediately in a louder murmur of voices, fading into far-off laughter, as the dark cloud swept away, leaving the clear and silent sky above Goodman Brown. But something fluttered lightly down through the air and caught on the branch of a tree. The young man seized it, and beheld a pink ribbon.

"My Faith is gone!" cried he, after one stupefied moment. "There is no good on earth; and sin is but a name. Come, devil; for to thee is this world given."

And, maddened with despair, so that he laughed loud and long, did Goodman Brown grasp his staff and set forth again, at such a rate that he seemed to fly along the forest path rather

than to walk or run. The road grew wilder and
drearier and more faintly traced, and vanished
at length, leaving him in the heart of the dark
wilderness, still rushing onward with the instinct that guides mortal man to evil. The whole
forest was peopled with frightful sounds — the
creaking of the trees, the howling of wild beasts,
and the yell of Indians; while sometimes the
wind tolled like a distant church bell, and sometimes gave a broad roar around the traveler, as
if all Nature were laughing him to scorn. But he
was himself the chief horror of the scene, and
shrank not from its other horrors.

"Ha! ha! ha!" roared Goodman Brown when
the wind laughed at him. "Let us hear which
will laugh loudest. Think not to frighten me
with your deviltry. Come witch, come wizard,
come Indian powwow, come devil himself, and
here comes Goodman Brown. You may as well
fear him as he fears you."

In truth, all through the haunted forest there
could be nothing more frightful than the figure
of Goodman Brown. On he flew among the
black pines, brandishing his staff with frenzied
gestures, now giving vent to an inspiration of
horrid blasphemy, and now shouting forth such
laughter as set all the echoes of the forest laughing like demons around him. The fiend in his
own shape is less hideous than when he rages in
the breast of man. Thus sped the demoniac on
his course, until, quivering among the trees, he
saw a red light before him, as when the felled
trunks and branches of a clearing have been set
on fire, and throw up their lurid blaze against

the sky, at the hour of midnight. He paused, in a lull of the tempest that had driven him onward, and heard the swell of what seemed a hymn, rolling solemnly from a distance with the weight of many voices. He knew the tune; it was a familiar one in the choir of the village meeting house. The verse died heavily away, and was lengthened by a chorus, not of human voices, but of all the sounds of the benighted wilderness pealing in awful harmony together. Goodman Brown cried out, and his cry was lost to his own ear by its unison with the cry of the desert.

In the interval of silence he stole forward until the light glared full upon his eyes. At one extremity of an open space, hemmed in by the dark wall of the forest, arose a rock, bearing some rude, natural resemblance either to an altar or a pulpit, and surrounded by four blazing pines, their tops aflame, their stems untouched, like candles at an evening meeting. The mass of foliage that had overgrown the summit of the rock was all on fire, blazing high into the night and fitfully illuminating the whole field. Each pendent twig and leafy festoon was in a blaze. As the red light arose and fell, a numerous congregation alternately shone forth, then disappeared in shadow, and again grew, as it were, out of the darkness, peopling the heart of the solitary woods at once.

"A grave and dark-clad company," quoth Goodman Brown.

In truth they were such. Among them, quivering to and fro between gloom and splendor, appeared faces that would be seen next day at

the council board of the province, and others
which, Sabbath after Sabbath, looked devoutly
heavenward, and benignantly over the crowded
pews, from the holiest pulpits in the land. Some
affirm that the lady of the governor was there.
At least there were high dames well known to
her, and wives of honored husbands, and widows, a great multitude, and ancient maidens, all
of excellent repute, and fair young girls, who
trembled lest their mothers should espy them.
Either the sudden gleams of light flashing over
the obscure field bedazzled Goodman Brown, or
he recognized a score of the church members of
Salem village famous for their especial sanctity.
Good old Deacon Gookin had arrived, and
waited at the skirts of that venerable saint, his
revered pastor. But, irreverently consorting
with these grave, reputable, and pious people,
these elders of the church, these chaste dames
and dewy virgins, there were men of dissolute
lives and women of spotted fame, wretches given
over to all mean and filthy vice, and suspected
even of horrid crimes. It was strange to see that
the good shrank not from the wicked, nor were
the sinners abashed by the saints. Scattered also
among their pale-faced enemies were the Indian
priests, or powwows, who had often scared their
native forest with more hideous incantations
than any known to English witchcraft.

"But where is Faith?" thought Goodman
Brown; and, as hope came into his heart, he
trembled.

Another verse of the hymn arose, a slow and
mournful strain, such as the pious love, but

joined to words which expressed all that our nature can conceive of sin, and darkly hinted at far more. Unfathomable to mere mortals is the lore of fiends. Verse after verse was sung; and still the chorus of the desert swelled between like the deepest tone of a mighty organ; and with the final peal of that dreadful anthem there came a sound, as if the roaring wind, the rushing streams, the howling beasts, and every other voice of the unconcerted wilderness were mingling and according with the voice of guilty man in homage to the prince of all. The four blazing pines threw up a loftier flame, and obscurely discovered shapes and visages of horror on the smoke wreaths above the impious assembly. At the same moment the fire on the rock shot redly forth and formed a glowing arch above its base, where now appeared a figure. With reverence be it spoken, the figure bore no slight similitude, both in garb and manner, to some grave divine of the New England churches.

"Bring forth the converts!" cried a voice that echoed through the field and rolled into the forest.

At the word, Goodman Brown stepped forth from the shadow of the trees and approached the congregation, with whom he felt a loathful brotherhood by the sympathy of all that was wicked in his heart. He could have well-nigh sworn that the shape of his own dead father beckoned him to advance, looking downward from a smoke wreath, while a woman, with dim features of despair, threw out her hand to warn him back. Was it his mother? But he had no power to retreat one step, nor to resist, even in thought, when the minister and good old Deacon Gookin seized his arms and led him to the blazing rock. Thither came also the slender form of a veiled female, led between Goody Cloyse, that pious teacher of the catechism, and Martha Carrier, who had received the devil's promise to be queen of hell. A rampant hag was she. And there stood the proselytes beneath the canopy of fire.

"Welcome, my children," said the dark figure, "to the communion of your race. Ye have found thus young your nature and your destiny. My children, look behind you!"

They turned; and flashing forth, as it were, in a sheet of flame, the fiend worshipers were seen; the smile of welcome gleamed darkly on every visage.

"There," resumed the sable form, "are all whom ye have reverenced from youth. Ye deemed them holier than yourselves, and shrank from your own sin, contrasting it with their lives of righteousness and prayerful aspirations heavenward. Yet here are they all in my worshiping assembly. This night it shall be granted you to know their secret deeds: how hoary-bearded elders of the church have whispered wanton words to the young maids of their households; how many a woman, eager for widows' weeds, has given her husband a drink at bedtime and let him sleep his last sleep in her bosom; how beardless youths have made haste to inherit their fathers' wealth; and how fair damsels — blush not, sweet ones — have dug lit-

tle graves in the garden, and bidden me, the sole
guest to an infant's funeral. By the sympathy of
your human hearts for sin ye shall scent out all
the places — whether in church, bedchamber,
street, field, or forest — where crime has been
committed, and shall exult to behold the whole
earth one stain of guilt, one mighty blood spot.
Far more than this. It shall be yours to penetrate, in every bosom, the deep mystery of sin,
the fountain of all wicked arts, and which in-
exhaustibly supplies more evil impulses than
human power — than my power at its utmost —
can make manifest in deeds. And now, my children, look upon each other."

They did so; and, by the blaze of the hell-
kindled torches, the wretched man beheld his
Faith, and the wife her husband, trembling before that unhallowed altar.

"Lo, there ye stand, my children," said the
figure, in a deep and solemn tone, almost sad
with its despairing awfulness, as if his once
angelic nature could yet mourn for our miserable race. "Depending upon one another's
hearts, ye had still hoped that virtue were not
all a dream. Now are ye undeceived. Evil is the
nature of mankind. Evil must be your only happiness. Welcome again, my children, to the communion of your race."

"Welcome," repeated the fiend worshipers, in
one cry of despair and triumph.

And there they stood, the only pair, as it
seemed, who were yet hesitating on the verge of
wickedness in this dark world. A basin was hol-
lowed, naturally, in the rock. Did it contain wa-

ter, reddened by the lurid light? or was it blood? or, perchance, a liquid flame? Herein did the shape of evil dip his hand and prepare to lay the mark of baptism upon their foreheads, that they might be partakers of the mystery of sin, more conscious of the secret guilt of others, both in deed and thought, than they could now be of their own. The husband cast one look at his pale wife, and Faith at him. What polluted wretches would the next glance show them to each other, shuddering alike at what they disclosed and what they saw!

"Faith! Faith!" cried the husband, "look up to heaven, and resist the wicked one."

Whether Faith obeyed he knew not. Hardly had he spoken when he found himself amid calm night and solitude, listening to a roar of the wind which died heavily away through the forest. He staggered against the rock, and felt it chill and damp; while a hanging twig, that had been all on fire, besprinkled his cheek with the coldest dew.

The next morning young Goodman Brown came slowly into the street of Salem village, staring around him like a bewildered man. The good old minister was taking a walk along the graveyard to get an appetite for breakfast and meditate his sermon, and bestowed a blessing, as he passed, on Goodman Brown. He shrank from the venerable saint as if to avoid an anathema. Old Deacon Gookin was at domestic worship, and the holy words of his prayer were heard through the open window. "What God doth the wizard pray to?" quoth Goodman

Brown. Goody Cloyse, that excellent old Christian, stood in the early sunshine at her own lattice, catechizing a little girl who had brought her a pint of morning's milk. Goodman Brown snatched away the child as from the grasp of the fiend himself. Turning the corner by the meetinghouse, he spied the head of Faith, with the pink ribbons, gazing anxiously forth, and bursting into such joy at sight of him that she skipped along the street and almost kissed her husband before the whole village. But Goodman Brown looked sternly and sadly into her face, and passed on without a greeting.

Had Goodman Brown fallen asleep in the forest and only dreamed a wild dream of a witch-meeting?

Be it so if you will; but, alas! it was a dream of evil omen for young Goodman Brown. A stern, a sad, a darkly meditative, a distrustful, if not a desperate man did he become from the night of that fearful dream. On the Sabbath day, when the congregation were singing a holy psalm, he could not listen because an anthem of sin rushed loudly upon his ear and drowned all the blessed strain. When the minister spoke from the pulpit with power and fervid eloquence, and, with his hand on the open Bible, of the sacred truths of our religion, and of saintlike lives and triumphant deaths, and of future bliss or misery unutterable, then did Goodman Brown turn pale, dreading lest the roof should thunder down upon the gray blasphemer and his hearers. Often, waking suddenly at midnight, he shrank from the bosom of

Faith; and at morning or eventide, when the family knelt down at prayer, he scowled and muttered to himself, and gazed sternly at his wife, and turned away. And when he had lived long, and was borne to his grave a hoary corpse, followed by Faith, an aged woman, and children and grandchildren, a goodly procession, besides neighbors not a few, they carved no hopeful verse upon his tombstone, for his dying hour was gloom.

THE MINISTER'S BLACK VEIL

A PARABLE*

THE SEXTON STOOD IN THE PORCH of Milford meetinghouse, pulling busily at the bell rope. The old people of the village came stooping along the street. Children, with bright faces, tripped merrily beside their parents, or mimicked a graver gait, in the conscious dignity of their Sunday clothes. Spruce bachelors looked sidelong at the pretty maidens, and fancied that the Sabbath sunshine made them prettier than

* Another clergyman in New England, Mr. Joseph Moody, of York, Maine, who died about eighty years since, made himself remarkable by the same eccentricity that is here related of the Reverend Mr. Hooper. In his case, however, the symbol had a different import. In early life he had accidentally killed a beloved friend; and from that day till the hour of his own death, he hid his face from men.

on week days. When the throng had mostly streamed into the porch, the sexton began to toll the bell, keeping his eye on the Reverend Mr. Hooper's door. The first glimpse of the clergyman's figure was the signal for the bell to cease its summons.

"But what has good Parson Hooper got upon his face?" cried the sexton in astonishment.

All within hearing immediately turned about, and beheld the semblance of Mr. Hooper, pacing slowly his meditative way toward the meetinghouse. With one accord they started, expressing more wonder than if some strange minister were coming to dust the cushions of Mr. Hooper's pulpit.

"Are you sure it is our parson?" inquired Goodman Gray of the sexton.

"Of a certainty it is good Mr. Hooper," replied the sexton. "He was to have exchanged pulpits with Parson Shute, of Westbury; but Parson Shute sent to excuse himself yesterday, being to preach a funeral sermon."

The cause of so much amazement may appear sufficiently slight. Mr. Hooper, a gentlemanly person, of about thirty, though still a bachelor, was dressed with due clerical neatness, as if a careful wife had starched his band, and brushed the weekly dust from his Sunday's garb. There was but one thing remarkable in his appearance. Swathed about his forehead, and hanging down over his face, so low as to be shaken by his breath, Mr. Hooper had on a black veil. On a nearer view it seemed to consist of two folds of crape, which entirely concealed his features, except the mouth and chin, but probably did not intercept his sight further than to give a darkened aspect to all living and inanimate things. With this gloomy shade before him, good Mr. Hooper walked onward, at a slow and quiet pace, stooping somewhat, and looking on the ground, as is customary with abstracted men, yet nodding kindly to those of his parishioners who still waited on the meetinghouse steps. But so wonder-struck were they that his greeting hardly met with a return.

"I can't really feel as if good Mr. Hooper's face was behind that piece of crape," said the sexton.

"I don't like it," muttered an old woman, as she hobbled into the meetinghouse. "He has changed himself into something awful, only by hiding his face."

"Our parson has gone mad!" cried Goodman Gray, following him across the threshold.

A rumor of some unaccountable phenomenon had preceded Mr. Hooper into the meetinghouse, and set all the congregation astir. Few could refrain from twisting their heads toward the door; many stood upright, and turned directly about; while several little boys clambered upon the seats, and came down again with a terrible racket. There was a general bustle, a rustling of the women's gowns and shuffling of the men's feet, greatly at variance with that hushed repose which should attend the entrance of the minister. But Mr. Hooper appeared not to notice the perturbation of his people. He entered with an almost noiseless step, bent his head mildly to the pews on each side, and bowed as he passed his oldest parishioner, a white-haired great grandsire, who occupied an arm-chair in the center of the aisle. It was strange to observe how slowly this venerable man became conscious of something singular in the appearance of his pastor. He seemed not fully to partake of the prevailing wonder, till Mr. Hooper had ascended the stairs, and showed himself in the pulpit, face to face with his congregation, except for the black veil. That mysterious emblem was never once with-drawn. It shook with his measured breath, as he gave out the psalm; it threw its obscurity be-tween him and the holy page as he read the Scriptures; and while he prayed, the veil lay heavily on his uplifted countenance. Did he seek to hide it from the dread Being whom he was addressing?

Such was the effect of this simple piece of crape, that more than one woman of delicate nerves was forced to leave the meetinghouse. Yet perhaps the palefaced congregation was al-most as fearful a sight to the minister, as his black veil to them.

Mr. Hooper had the reputation of a good preacher, but not an energetic one: he strove to win his people heavenward by mild, persuasive influences, rather than to drive them thither by the thunders of the Word. The sermon which he now delivered was marked by the same charac-teristics of style and manner as the general se-ries of his pulpit oratory. But there was some-thing, either in the sentiment of the discourse itself, or in the imagination of the auditors, which made it greatly the most powerful effort that they had ever heard from their pastor's lips. It was tinged, rather more darkly than usual, with the gentle gloom of Mr. Hooper's temperament. The subject had reference to secret sin, and those sad mysteries which we hide from our nearest and dearest, and would fain conceal from our own consciousness, even forgetting that the Omniscient can detect them. A subtle power was breathed into his words. Each member of the congregation, the most innocent girl and the man of hardened breast, felt as if the preacher had crept upon them, behind his awful veil, and discovered their hoarded iniquity of deed or thought. Many spread their clasped hands on their bosoms. There was nothing terrible in what Mr. Hooper said, at least, no violence; and yet, with every tremor of his melancholy voice, the hearers quaked. An unsought pathos came hand in hand with awe. So sensible were the audience of some unwonted attribute in their minister, that they longed for a breath of wind to blow aside the veil, almost believing that a stranger's visage would be discovered, though the form, gesture, and voice were those of Mr. Hooper.

At the close of the services, the people hurried out with indecorous confusion, eager to communicate their pent-up amazement, and conscious of lighter spirits the moment they lost sight of the black veil. Some gathered in little circles, huddled closely together, with their mouths all whispering in the center; some went homeward alone, wrapt in silent meditation; some talked loudly, and profaned the Sabbath day with ostentatious laughter. A few shook their sagacious heads, intimating that they could penetrate the mystery; while one or two affirmed that there was no mystery at all, but only that Mr. Hooper's eyes were so weakened by the midnight lamp, as to require a shade. After a brief interval, forth came good Mr. Hooper also, in the rear of his flock. Turning his veiled face from one group to another, he paid due reverence to the hoary heads, saluted the middle-aged with kind dignity as their friend and spiritual guide, greeted the young with mingled authority and love, and laid his hands on the little children's heads to bless them. Such was always his custom on the Sabbath day. Strange and bewildered looks repaid him for his courtesy. None, as on former occasions, aspired to the honor of walking by their pastor's side. Old Squire Saunders, doubtless by an accidental lapse of memory, neglected to invite Mr. Hooper to his table, where the good clergyman had been wont to bless the food, almost every Sunday since his settlement. He returned, therefore, to the parsonage, and, at the moment of closing the door, was observed to look back upon the people, all of whom had their eyes fixed upon the minister. A sad smile gleamed faintly from beneath the black veil, and flickered about his mouth, glimmering as he disappeared.

"How strange," said a lady, "that a simple black veil, such as any woman might wear on her bonnet, should become such a terrible thing on Mr. Hooper's face!"

"Something must surely be amiss with Mr. Hooper's intellects," observed her husband, the physician of the village. "But the strangest part of the affair is the effect of this vagary, even on a sober-minded man like myself. The black veil, though it covers only our pastor's face, throws its influence over his whole person, and makes him ghostlike from head to foot. Do you not feel it so?"

"Truly do I," replied the lady; "and I would not be alone with him for the world. I wonder he is not afraid to be alone with himself!"

"Men sometimes are so," said her husband.

The afternoon service was attended with similar circumstances. At its conclusion, the bell tolled for the funeral of a young lady. The relatives and friends were assembled in the house, and the more distant acquaintances stood about the door, speaking of the good qualities of the deceased, when their talk was interrupted by the appearance of Mr. Hooper, still covered with his black veil. It was now an appropriate emblem. The clergyman stepped into the room where the corpse was laid, and bent over the coffin, to take a last farewell of his deceased parishioner. As he stooped, the veil hung straight down from his forehead, so that, if her eyelids had not been closed forever, the dead maiden might have seen his face. Could Mr. Hooper be fearful of her glance, that he so hastily caught back the black veil? A person who watched the interview between the dead and living, scru-

pled not to affirm, that, at the instant when the
clergyman's features were disclosed, the corpse
had slightly shuddered, rustling the shroud and
muslin cap, though the countenance retained
the composure of death. A superstitious old
woman was the only witness of this prodigy.
From the coffin Mr. Hooper passed into the
chamber of the mourners, and thence to the
head of the staircase, to make the funeral prayer.
It was a tender and heart-dissolving prayer, full
of sorrow, yet so imbued with celestial hopes,
that the music of a heavenly harp, swept by the
fingers of the dead, seemed faintly to be heard
among the saddest accents of the minister. The
people trembled, though they but darkly understood him when he prayed that they, and himself, and all of mortal race, might be ready, as
he trusted this young maiden had been, for the
dreadful hour that should snatch the veil from
their faces. The bearers went heavily forth, and
the mourners followed, saddening all the street,
with the dead before them, and Mr. Hooper in
his black veil behind.

"Why do you look back?" said one in the procession to his partner.

"I had a fancy," replied she, "that the minister and the maiden's spirit were walking hand
in hand."

"And so had I, at the same moment," said the
other.

That night, the handsomest couple in Milford
village were to be joined in wedlock. Though
reckoned a melancholy man, Mr. Hooper had
a placid cheerfulness for such occasions, which

often excited a sympathetic smile where live-
lier merriment would have been thrown away.
There was no quality of his disposition which
made him more beloved than this. The company at the wedding awaited his arrival with im-
patience, trusting that the strange awe, which
had gathered over him throughout the day,
would now be dispelled. But such was not
the result. When Mr. Hooper came, the first
thing that their eyes rested on was the same horrible black veil, which had added deeper gloom
to the funeral, and could portend nothing but
evil to the wedding. Such was its immediate effect on the guests that a cloud seemed to have
rolled duskily from beneath the black crape, and
dimmed the light of the candles. The bridal pair
stood up before the minister. But the bride's
cold fingers quivered in the tremulous hand of
the bridegroom, and her deathlike paleness
caused a whisper that the maiden who had been
buried a few hours before was come from her
grave to be married. If ever another wedding
were so dismal, it was that famous one where
they tolled the wedding knell. After performing
the ceremony, Mr. Hooper raised a glass of wine
to his lips, wishing happiness to the new married
couple in a strain of mild pleasantry that ought
to have brightened the features of the guests,
like a cheerful gleam from the hearth. At that
instant, catching a glimpse of his figure in the
looking glass, the black veil involved his own
spirit in the horror with which it overwhelmed
all others. His frame shuddered, his lips grew
white, he spilt the untasted wine upon the car-

pet, and rushed forth into the darkness. For the
Earth, too, had on her Black Veil.

The next day, the whole village of Milford
talked of little else than Parson Hooper's black
veil. That, and the mystery concealed behind it,
supplied a topic for discussion between acquaintances meeting in the street, and good
women gossiping at their open windows. It was
the first item of news that the tavern-keeper told
to his guests. The children babbled of it on their
way to school. One imitative little imp covered
his face with an old black handkerchief thereby
so affrighting his playmates that the panic seized
himself, and he well-nigh lost his wits by his own
waggery.

It was remarkable that of all the busybodies
and impertinent people in the parish, not one
ventured to put the plain question to Mr.
Hooper, wherefore he did this thing. Hitherto,
whenever there appeared the slightest call for
such interference, he had never lacked advisers,
nor shown himself averse to be guided by their
judgment. If he erred at all, it was by so painful
a degree of self-distrust, that even the mildest
censure would lead him to consider an indifferent action as a crime. Yet, though so well
acquainted with this amiable weakness, no individual among his parishioners chose to make
the black veil a subject of friendly remonstrance. There was a feeling of dread, neither
plainly confessed nor carefully concealed, which
caused each to shift the responsibility upon another, till at length it was found expedient to
send a deputation of the church, in order to

deal with Mr. Hooper about the mystery, before it should grow into a scandal. Never did an
embassy so ill discharge its duties. The minister
received them with friendly courtesy, but became silent, after they were seated, leaving to
his visitors the whole burden of introducing
their important business. The topic, it might
be supposed, was obvious enough. There was
the black veil swathed round Mr. Hooper's forehead, and concealing every feature above his
placid mouth, on which, at times, they could
perceive the glimmering of a melancholy smile.
But that piece of crape, to their imagination,
seemed to hang down before his heart, the symbol of a fearful secret between him and them.
Were the veil but cast aside, they might speak
freely of it, but not till then. Thus they sat a
considerable time, speechless, confused, and
shrinking uneasily from Mr. Hooper's eye,
which they felt to be fixed upon them with an
invisible glance. Finally, the deputies returned
abashed to their constituents, pronouncing the
matter too weighty to be handled, except by a
council of the churches, if, indeed, it might not
require a general synod.

But there was one person in the village unap-
palled by the awe with which the black veil had
impressed all beside herself. When the deputies
returned without an explanation, or even ven-
turing to demand one, she, with the calm energy
of her character, determined to chase away the
strange cloud that appeared to be settling round
Mr. Hooper, every moment more darkly than
before. As his plighted wife, it should be her

privilege to know what the black veil concealed. At the minister's first visit, therefore, she entered upon the subject with a direct simplicity, which made the task easier both for him and her. After he had seated himself, she fixed her eyes steadfastly upon the veil, but could discern nothing of the dreadful gloom that had so overawed the multitude: it was but a double fold of crape, hanging down from his forehead to his mouth, and slightly stirring with his breath.

"No," said she aloud, and smiling, "there is nothing terrible in this piece of crape, except that it hides a face which I am always glad to look upon. Come, good sir, let the sun shine from behind the cloud. First lay aside your black veil: then tell me why you put it on."

Mr. Hooper's smile glimmered faintly.

"There is an hour to come," said he, "when all of us shall cast aside our veils. Take it not amiss, beloved friend, if I wear this piece of crape till then."

"Your words are a mystery, too," returned the young lady. "Take away the veil from them, at least."

"Elizabeth, I will," said he, "so far as my vow may suffer me. Know, then, this veil is a type and a symbol, and I am bound to wear it ever, both in light and darkness, in solitude and before the gaze of multitudes, and as with strangers, so with my familiar friends. No mortal eye will see it withdrawn. This dismal shade must separate me from the world: even you, Elizabeth, can never come behind it!"

"What grievous affliction hath befallen you,"

she earnestly inquired, "that you should thus darken your eyes forever?"

"If it be a sign of mourning," replied Mr. Hooper, "I, perhaps, like most other mortals, have sorrows dark enough to be typified by a black veil."

"But what if the world will not believe that it is the type of an innocent sorrow?" urged Elizabeth. "Beloved and respected as you are, there may be whispers that you hide your face under the consciousness of secret sin. For the sake of your holy office, do away this scandal!"

The color rose into her cheeks as she intimated the nature of the rumors that were already abroad in the village. But Mr. Hooper's mildness did not forsake him. He even smiled again — that same sad smile, which always appeared like a faint glimmering of light, proceeding from the obscurity beneath the veil.

"If I hide my face for sorrow, there is cause enough," he merely replied; "and if I cover it for secret sin, what mortal might not do the same?"

And with this gentle, but unconquerable obstinacy did he resist all her entreaties. At length Elizabeth sat silent. For a few moments she appeared lost in thought, considering, probably, what new methods might be tried to withdraw her lover from so dark a fantasy, which, if it had no other meaning, was perhaps a symptom of mental disease. Though of a firmer character than his own, the tears rolled down her cheeks. But, in an instant, as it were, a new feeling took the place of sorrow: her eyes were fixed insen-

sibly on the black veil, when, like a sudden twilight in the air, its terrors fell around her. She
arose, and stood trembling before him.

"And do you feel it then, at last?" said he
mournfully.

She made no reply, but covered her eyes with
her hand, and turned to leave the room. He
rushed forward and caught her arm.

"Have patience with me, Elizabeth!" cried he,
passionately. "Do not desert me, though this
veil must be between us here on earth. Be mine,
and hereafter there shall be no veil over my face,
no darkness between our souls! It is but a mortal
veil — it is not for eternity! O! you know not
how lonely I am, and how frightened, to be
alone behind my black veil. Do not leave me
in this miserable obscurity forever!"

"Lift the veil but once, and look me in the
face," said she.

"Never! It cannot be!" replied Mr. Hooper.

"Then farewell!" said Elizabeth.

She withdrew her arm from his grasp, and
slowly departed, pausing at the door, to give one
long shuddering gaze, that seemed almost to
penetrate the mystery of the black veil. But,
even amid his grief, Mr. Hooper smiled to think
that only a material emblem had separated him
from happiness, though the horrors, which it
shadowed forth, must be drawn darkly between
the fondest of lovers.

From that time no attempts were made to remove Mr. Hooper's black veil, or, by a direct
appeal, to discover the secret which it was supposed to hide. By persons who claimed a superi-

ority to popular prejudice, it was reckoned merely an eccentric whim, such as often mingles with the sober actions of men otherwise rational, and tinges them all with its own semblance of insanity. But with the multitude, good Mr. Hooper was irreparably a bugbear. He could not walk the street with any peace of mind, so conscious was he that the gentle and timid would turn aside to avoid him, and that others would make it a point of hardihood to throw themselves in his way. The impertinence of the latter class compelled him to give up his customary walk at sunset to the burial ground; for when he leaned pensively over the gate, there would always be faces behind the gravestones, peeping at his black veil. A fable went the rounds that the stare of the dead people drove him thence. It grieved him, to the very depth of his kind heart, to observe how the children fled from his approach, breaking up their merriest sports, while his melancholy figure was yet afar off. Their instinctive dread caused him to feel more strongly than aught else, that a preternatural horror was interwoven with the threads of the black crape. In truth, his own antipathy to the veil was known to be so great, that he never willingly passed before a mirror, nor stooped to drink at a still fountain, lest, in its peaceful bosom, he should be affrighted by himself. This was what gave plausibility to the whispers, that Mr. Hooper's conscience tortured him for some great crime too horrible to be entirely concealed, or otherwise than so obscurely intimated. Thus, from

beneath the black veil, there rolled a cloud into
the sunshine, an ambiguity of sin or sorrow,
which enveloped the poor minister, so that love
or sympathy could never reach him. It was said
that ghost and fiend consorted with him there.
With self-shudderings and outward terrors, he
walked continually in its shadow, groping
darkly within his own soul, or gazing through
a medium that saddened the whole world. Even
the lawless wind, it was believed, respected his
dreadful secret, and never blew aside the veil.
But still good Mr. Hooper sadly smiled at the
pale visages of the worldly throng as he passed
by.

Among all its bad influences, the black veil
had the one desirable effect, of making its
wearer a very efficient clergyman. By the aid of
his mysterious emblem — for there was no other
apparent cause — he became a man of awful
power over souls that were in agony for sin. His
converts always regarded him with a dread peculiar to themselves, affirming, though but figuratively, that, before he brought them to celestial
light, they had been with him behind the black
veil. Its gloom, indeed, enabled him to sym-
pathize with all dark affections. Dying sinners
cried aloud for Mr. Hooper, and would not
yield their breath till he appeared; though ever,
as he stooped to whisper consolation, they shuddered at the veiled face so near their own. Such
were the terrors of the black veil, even when
Death had bared his visage! Strangers came long
distances to attend service at his church, with
the mere idle purpose of gazing at his figure,

because it was forbidden them to behold his face. But many were made to quake ere they departed! Once, during Governor Belcher's administration, Mr. Hooper was appointed to preach the election sermon. Covered with his black veil, he stood before the chief magistrate, the council, and the representatives, and wrought so deep an impression, that the legislative measures of that year were characterized by all the gloom and piety of our earliest ancestral sway.

In this manner Mr. Hooper spent a long life, irreproachable in outward act, yet shrouded in dismal suspicions; kind and loving, though unloved, and dimly feared; a man apart from men, shunned in their health and joy, but ever summoned to their aid in mortal anguish. As years wore on, shedding their snows above his sable veil, he acquired a name throughout the New England churches, and they called him Father Hooper. Nearly all his parishioners, who were of mature age when he was settled, had been borne away by many a funeral: he had one congregation in the church, and a more crowded one in the churchyard; and having wrought so late into the evening, and done his work so well, it was now good Father Hooper's turn to rest.

Several persons were visible by the shaded candlelight, in the death chamber of the old clergyman. Natural connections he had none. But there was the decorously grave, though unmoved physician, seeking only to mitigate the last pangs of the patient whom he could not save. There were the deacons, and other eminently pious members of his church. There, also, was the Reverend Mr. Clark, of Westbury, a young and zealous divine, who had ridden in haste to pray by the bedside of the expiring minister. There was the nurse, no hired handmaiden of death, but one whose calm affection had endured thus long in secrecy, in solitude, amid the chill of age, and would not perish, even at the dying hour. Who, but Elizabeth! And there lay the hoary head of good Father Hooper upon the death pillow, with the black veil still swathed about his brow, and reaching down over his face, so that each more difficult gasp of his faint breath caused it to stir. All through life that piece of crape had hung between him and the world: it had separated him from cheerful brotherhood and woman's love, and kept him in that saddest of all prisons, his own heart; and still it lay upon his face, as if to deepen the gloom of his darksome chamber, and shade him from the sunshine of eternity.

For some time previous, his mind had been confused, wavering doubtfully between the past and the present, and hovering forward, as it were, at intervals, into the indistinctness of the world to come. There had been feverish turns, which tossed him from side to side, and wore away what little strength he had. But in his most convulsive struggles, and in the wildest vagaries of his intellect, when no other thought retained its sober influence, he still showed an awful solicitude lest the black veil should slip aside. Even if his bewildered soul could have forgotten, there was a faithful woman at his

pillow, who, with averted eyes, would have covered that aged face, which she had last beheld
in the comeliness of manhood. At length the
death-stricken old man lay quietly in the torpor
of mental and bodily exhaustion, with an im-
perceptible pulse, and breath that grew fainter
and fainter, except when a long, deep, and irregular inspiration seemed to prelude the flight
of his spirit.

The minister of Westbury approached the
bedside.

"Venerable Father Hooper," said he, "the
moment of your release is at hand. Are you
ready for the lifting of the veil that shuts in time
from eternity?"

Father Hooper at first replied merely by a
feeble motion of his head; then, apprehensive,
perhaps, that his meaning might be doubted,
he exerted himself to speak.

"Yea," said he, in faint accents, "my soul hath
a patient weariness until that veil be lifted."

"And is it fitting," resumed the Reverend
Mr. Clark, "that a man so given to prayer, of
such a blameless example, holy in deed and
thought, so far as mortal judgment may pronounce; is it fitting that a father in the church
should leave a shadow on his memory, that may
seem to blacken a life so pure? I pray you, my
venerable brother, let not this thing be! Suffer
us to be gladdened by your triumphant aspect
as you go to your reward. Before the veil of
eternity be lifted, let me cast aside this black
veil from your face!"

And thus speaking, the Reverend Mr. Clark

bent forward to reveal the mystery of so many years. But, exerting a sudden energy, that made all the beholders stand aghast, Father Hooper snatched both his hands from beneath the bedclothes, and pressed them strongly on the black veil, resolute to struggle, if the minister of Westbury would contend with a dying man.

"Never!" cried the veiled clergyman. "On earth, never!"

"Dark old man!" exclaimed the affrighted minister, "with what horrible crime upon your soul are you now passing to the judgment?"

Father Hooper's breath heaved; it rattled in his throat; but, with a mighty effort, grasping forward with his hands, he caught hold of life, and held it back till he should speak. He even raised himself in bed; and there he sat, shivering with the arms of death around him, while the black veil hung down, awful, at that last moment, in the gathered terrors of a lifetime. And yet the faint, sad smile, so often there, now seemed to glimmer from its obscurity, and linger on Father Hooper's lips.

"Why do you tremble at me alone?" cried he, turning his veiled face round the circle of pale spectators. "Tremble also at each other! Have men avoided me, and women shown no pity, and children screamed and fled, only for my black veil? What, but the mystery which it obscurely typifies, has made this piece of crape so awful? When the friend shows his inmost heart to his friend; the lover to his best beloved; when man does not vainly shrink from the eye of his Creator, loathsomely treasuring up the secret of his sin; then deem me a monster, for the symbol beneath which I have lived, and die! I look around me, and, lo! on every visage a Black Veil!"

While his auditors shrank from one another, in mutual affright, Father Hooper fell back upon his pillow, a veiled corpse, with a faint smile lingering on the lips. Still veiled, they laid him in his coffin, and a veiled corpse they bore him to the grave. The grass of many years has sprung up and withered on that grave, the burial stone is moss-grown, and good Mr. Hooper's face is dust; but awful is still the thought that it moldered beneath the Black Veil!

FEATHERTOP: A MORALIZED LEGEND

"DICKON," CRIED MOTHER RIGBY, "a coal for my pipe!"

The pipe was in the old dame's mouth when she said these words. She had thrust it there after filling it with tobacco, but without stooping to light it at the hearth, where indeed there was no appearance of a fire having been kindled that morning. Forthwith, however, as soon as the order was given, there was an intense red glow out of the bowl of the pipe, and a whiff of smoke came from Mother Rigby's lips. Whence the coal came, and how brought thither by an invisible hand, I have never been able to discover.

"Good!" quoth Mother Rigby, with a nod of her head. "Thank ye, Dickon! And now for making this scarecrow. Be within call, Dickon, in case I need you again."

The good woman had risen thus early (for as yet it was scarcely sunrise) in order to set about making a scarecrow, which she intended to put in the middle of her cornpatch. It was now the latter week of May, and the crows and black-birds had already discovered the little, green, rolled-up leaf of the Indian corn just peeping out of the soil. She was determined, therefore, to contrive as lifelike a scarecrow as ever was seen, and to finish it immediately, from top to toe, so that it should begin its sentinel's duty that very morning. Now Mother Rigby (as everybody must have heard) was one of the most cunning and potent witches in New England, and might, with very little trouble, have made a scarecrow ugly enough to frighten the minister himself. But on this occasion, as she had awak-ened in an uncommonly pleasant humor, and was further dulcified by her pipe tobacco, she resolved to produce something fine, beautiful, and splendid, rather than hideous and horrible.

"I don't want to set up a hobgoblin in my own cornpatch, and almost at my own doorstep," said Mother Rigby to herself, puffing out a whiff of smoke; "I could do it if I pleased, but I'm tired of doing marvelous things, and so I'll keep within the bounds of everyday business just for variety's sake. Besides, there is no use in scaring the little children for a mile roundabout, though 'tis true I'm a witch."

It was settled, therefore, in her own mind, that the scarecrow should represent a fine gen-tleman of the period, so far as the materials at hand would allow. Perhaps it may be as well to enumerate the chief of the articles that went to the composition of this figure.

The most important item of all, probably, although it made so little show, was a certain broomstick, on which Mother Rigby had taken many an airy gallop at midnight, and which now served the scarecrow by way of a spinal column, or, as the unlearned phrase it, a backbone. One of its arms was a disabled flail which used to be wielded by Goodman Rigby, before his spouse worried him out of this troublesome world; the other, if I mistake not, was composed of the pudding stick and a broken rung of a chair, tied loosely together at the elbow. As for its legs, the right was a hoe handle, and the left an undistinguished and miscellaneous stick from the woodpile. Its lungs, stomach, and other affairs of that kind were nothing better than a meal bag stuffed with straw. Thus we have made out the skeleton and entire corporosity of the scarecrow, with the exception of its head; and this was admirably supplied by a somewhat withered and shriveled pumpkin, in which Mother Rigby cut two holes for the eyes, and a slit for the mouth, leaving a bluish-colored knob in the middle to pass for a nose. It was really quite a respectable face.

"I've seen worse ones on human shoulders, at any rate," said Mother Rigby. "And many a fine gentleman has a pumpkin head, as well as my scarecrow."

But the clothes, in this case, were to be the making of the man. So the good old woman took down from a peg an ancient plum-colored

coat of London make, and with relics of embroidery on its seams, cuffs, pocket flaps, and
buttonholes, but lamentably worn and faded,
patched at the elbows, tattered at the skirts, and
threadbare all over. On the left breast was a
round hole, whence either a star of nobility
had been rent away, or else the hot heart of some
former wearer had scorched it through and
through. The neighbors said that this rich garment belonged to the Black Man's wardrobe,
and that he kept it at Mother Rigby's cottage
for the convenience of slipping it on whenever
he wished to make a grand appearance at the
governor's table. To match the coat there was a
velvet waistcoat of very ample size, and formerly
embroidered with foliage that had been as
brightly golden as the maple leaves in October,
but which had now quite vanished out of
the substance of the velvet. Next came a pair of
scarlet breeches, once worn by the French
governor of Louisbourg, and the knees of
which had touched the lower step of the throne
of Louis le Grand. The Frenchman had given
these smallclothes to an Indian powwow, who
parted with them to the old witch for a gill
of strong waters, at one of their dances in the
forest. Furthermore, Mother Rigby produced a
pair of silk stockings and put them on the figure's legs, where they showed as unsubstantial
as a dream, with the wooden reality of the two
sticks making itself miserably apparent through
the holes. Lastly, she put her dead husband's
wig on the bare scalp of the pumpkin, and sur-
mounted the whole with a dusty three-cornered

hat, in which was stuck the longest tail feather of a rooster.

Then the old dame stood the figure up in a corner of her cottage and chuckled to behold its yellow semblance of a visage, with its nobby little nose thrust into the air. It had a strangely self-satisfied aspect, and seemed to say, "Come look at me!"

"And you are well worth looking at, that's a fact!" quoth Mother Rigby, in admiration at her own handiwork. "I've made many a puppet since I've been a witch, but methinks this is the finest of them all. 'Tis almost too good for a scarecrow. And, by the by, I'll just fill a fresh pipe of tobacco and then take him out to the cornpatch."

While filling her pipe the old woman continued to gaze with almost motherly affection at the figure in the corner. To say the truth, whether it were chance, or skill, or downright witchcraft, there was something wonderfully human in this ridiculous shape, bedizened with its tattered finery; and as for the countenance, it appeared to shrivel its yellow surface into a grin — a funny kind of expression betwixt scorn and merriment, as if it understood itself to be a jest at mankind. The more Mother Rigby looked the better she was pleased.

"Dickon," cried she sharply, "another coal for my pipe!"

Hardly had she spoken, then, just as before, there was a red-glowing coal on the top of the tobacco. She drew in a long whiff and puffed it forth again into the bar of morning sunshine which struggled through the one dusty pane of her cottage window. Mother Rigby always liked to flavor her pipe with a coal of fire from the particular chimney corner whence this had been brought. But where that chimney corner might be, or who brought the coal from it — further than that the invisible messenger seemed to respond to the name of Dickon — I cannot tell.

"That puppet yonder," thought Mother Rigby, still with her eyes fixed on the scarecrow, "is too good a piece of work to stand all summer in a cornpatch, frightening away the crows and blackbirds. He's capable of better things. Why, I've danced with a worse one, when partners happened to be scarce, at our witch meetings in the forest! What if I should let him take his chance among the other men of straw and empty fellows who go bustling about the world?"

The old witch took three or four more whiffs of her pipe and smiled.

"He'll meet plenty of his brethren at every street corner!" continued she. "Well; I didn't mean to dabble in witchcraft today, further than the lighting of my pipe, but a witch I am, and a witch I'm likely to be, and there's no use trying to shirk it. I'll make a man of my scarecrow, were it only for the joke's sake!"

While muttering these words, Mother Rigby took the pipe from her own mouth and thrust it into the crevice which represented the same feature in the pumpkin visage of the scarecrow.

"Puff, darling, puff!" said she. "Puff away, my fine fellow! Your life depends on it!"

This was a strange exhortation, undoubtedly,

to be addressed to a mere thing of sticks, straw, and old clothes, with nothing better than a shriveled pumpkin for a head — as we know to have been the scarecrow's case. Nevertheless, as we must carefully hold in remembrance, Mother Rigby was a witch of singular power and dexterity; and, keeping this fact duly before our minds, we shall see nothing beyond credibility in the remarkable incidents of our story. Indeed, the great difficulty will be at once got over, if we can only bring ourselves to believe that, as soon as the old dame bade him puff, there came a whiff of smoke from the scarecrow's mouth. It was the very feeblest of whiffs, to be sure; but it was followed by another and another, each more decided than the preceding one.

"Puff away, my pet! Puff away, my pretty one!" Mother Rigby kept repeating, with her pleasantest smile. "It is the breath of life to ye; and that you may take my word for."

Beyond all question the pipe was bewitched. There must have been a spell either in the tobacco or in the fiercely glowing coal that so mysteriously burned on top of it, or in the pungently aromatic smoke which exhaled from the kindled weed. The figure, after a few doubtful attempts, at length blew forth a volley of smoke extending all the way from the obscure corner into the bar of sunshine. There it eddied and melted away among the motes of dust. It seemed a convulsive effort; for the two or three next whiffs were fainter, although the coal still glowed and threw a gleam over the scarecrow's visage. The old witch clapped her skinny hands together, and smiled encouragingly upon her handiwork. She saw that the charm worked well. The shriveled, yellow face, which heretofore had been no face at all, had already a thin, fantastic haze, as it were of human likeness, shifting to and fro across it; sometimes vanishing entirely, but growing more perceptible than ever with the next whiff from the pipe. The whole figure, in like manner, assumed a show of life, such as we impart to ill-defined shapes among the clouds, and half deceive ourselves with the pastime of our own fancy.

If we must needs pry closely into the matter, it may be doubted whether there was any real change, after all, in the sordid, wornout, worthless, and ill-jointed substance of the scarecrow; but merely a spectral illusion, and a cunning effect of light and shade so colored and contrived as to delude the eyes of most men. The miracles of witchcraft seem always to have had a very shallow subtlety; and, at least, if the above explanations do not hit the truth of the process, I can suggest no better.

"Well puffed, my pretty lad!" still cried old Mother Rigby. "Come, another good stout whiff, and let it be with might and main. Puff for thy life, I tell thee! Puff out of the very bottom of thy heart, if any heart thou hast, or any bottom to it! Well done, again! Thou didst suck in that mouthful as if for the pure love of it."

And then the witch beckoned to the scarecrow, throwing so much magnetic potency into her gesture that it seemed as if it must inevitably be obeyed, like the mystic call of the loadstone when it summons the iron.

"Why lurkest thou in the corner, lazy one?" said she. "Step forth. Thou hast the world before thee!"

Upon my word, if the legend were not one which I heard on my grandmother's knee, and which had established its place among things credible before my childish judgment could analyze its probability, I question whether I should have the face to tell it now.

In obedience to Mother Rigby's word, and extending its arm as if to reach her outstretched hand, the figure made a step forward — a kind of hitch and jerk, however, rather than a step —then tottered and almost lost its balance. What could the witch expect? It was nothing, after all, but a scarecrow stuck upon two sticks. But the strong-willed old beldam scowled, and beckoned, and flung the energy of her purpose so forcibly at this poor combination of rotten wood, and musty straw, and ragged garments, that it was compelled to show itself a man, in spite of the reality of things. So it stepped into the bar of sunshine. There it stood — poor devil of a contrivance that it was! — with only the thinnest vesture of human similitude about it, through which was evident the stiff, rickety, incongruous, faded, tattered, good-for-nothing patchwork of its substance, ready to sink in a heap upon the floor, as conscious of its own unworthiness to be erect. Shall I confess the truth? At its present point of vivification, the scarecrow reminds me of some of the lukewarm and abortive characters, composed of heterogeneous materials, used for the thousandth time, and never worth using, with which romance writers (and myself, no doubt, among the rest) have so over-peopled the world of fiction.

But the fierce old hag began to get angry and show a glimpse of her diabolic nature (like a snake's head, peeping with a hiss out of her bosom), at this pusillanimous behavior of the thing which she had taken the trouble to put together.

"Puff away, wretch!" cried she, wrathfully. "Puff, puff, puff, thou thing of straw and emptiness! thou rag or two! thou meal bag! thou pumpkin head! thou nothing! Where shall I find a name vile enough to call thee by? Puff, I say, and suck in thy fantastic life with the smoke! Else I snatch the pipe from thy mouth and hurl thee where that red coal came from."

Thus threatened, the unhappy scarecrow had nothing for it but to puff away for dear life. As need was, therefore, it applied itself lustily to the pipe, and sent forth such abundant volleys of tobacco smoke that the small cottage kitchen became all vaporous. The one sunbeam struggled mistily through, and could but imperfectly define the image of the cracked and dusty window pane on the opposite wall. Mother Rigby meanwhile, with one brown arm akimbo and the other stretched toward the figure, loomed grimly amid the obscurity with such port and expression as when she was wont to heave a ponderous nightmare on her victims and stand at the bedside to enjoy their agony. In fear and trembling did this poor scarecrow puff. But its efforts, it must be acknowledged, served an excellent purpose; for, with each successive whiff, the figure lost more and more of its dizzy and perplexing tenuity and seemed to take denser substance. Its very garments, moreover, partook of the magical change, and shone with the gloss of novelty and glistened with the skillfully embroidered gold that had long ago been rent away. And, half revealed among the smoke, a yellow visage bent its lusterless eyes on Mother Rigby.

At last the old witch clinched her fist and shook it at the figure. Not that she was positively angry, but merely acting on the principle — perhaps untrue, or not the only truth, though as high a one as Mother Rigby could be expected to attain — that feeble and torpid natures, being incapable of better inspiration, must be stirred up by fear. But here was the crisis. Should she fail in what she now sought to effect, it was her ruthless purpose to scatter the miserable simulacre into its original elements.

"Thou hast a man's aspect," said she, sternly. "Have also the echo and mockery of a voice! I bid thee speak!"

The scarecrow gasped, struggled, and at length emitted a murmur, which was so incorporated with its smoky breath that you could scarcely tell whether it were indeed a voice or only a whiff of tobacco. Some narrators of this legend hold the opinion that Mother Rigby's conjurations and the fierceness of her will had compelled a familiar spirit into the figure, and that the voice was his.

"Mother," mumbled the poor stifled voice, "be not so awful with me! I would fain speak; but being without wits, what can I say?"

"Thou canst speak, darling, canst thou?" cried Mother Rigby, relaxing her grim countenance into a smile. "And what shalt thou say, quotha! Say, indeed! Art thou of the brotherhood of the empty skull, and demandest of me what thou shalt say? Thou shalt say a thousand things, and saying them a thousand times over, thou shalt still have said nothing! Be not afraid, I tell thee! When thou comest into the world (whither I purpose sending thee forthwith) thou shalt not lack the wherewithal to talk. Talk! Why, thou shall babble like a millstream, if thou wilt. Thou hast brains enough for that, I trow!"

"At your service, mother," responded the figure.

"And that was well said, my pretty one," answered Mother Rigby. "Then thou speakest like thyself, and meant nothing. Thou shalt have a hundred such set phrases, and five hundred to the boot of them. And now, darling, I have taken so much pains with thee and thou art so beautiful, that, by my troth, I love thee better than any witch's puppet in the world; and I've made them of all sorts — clay, wax, straw, sticks, night fog, morning mist, sea foam, and chimney smoke. But thou art the very best. So give heed to what I say."

"Yes, kind mother," said the figure, "with all my heart!"

"With all thy heart!" cried the old witch, setting her hands to her sides and laughing loudly. "Thou hast such a pretty way of speaking. With all thy heart! And thou didst put thy hand to the left side of thy waistcoat as if thou really hadst one!"

So now, in high good humor with this fantastic contrivance of hers, Mother Rigby told the scarecrow that it must go and play its part in the great world, where not one man in a hundred, she affirmed, was gifted with more real substance than itself. And, that he might hold up his head with the best of them, she endowed him, on the spot, with an unreckonable amount of wealth. It consisted partly of a gold mine in Eldorado, and of ten thousand shares in a broken bubble, and of half a million acres of vineyard at the North Pole, and of a castle in the air, and a chateau in Spain, together with all the rents and income therefrom accruing. She further made over to him the cargo of a certain ship, laden with salt of Cadiz, which she herself, by her necromantic arts, had caused to founder, ten years before, in the deepest part of mid-ocean. If the salt were not dissolved, and could be brought to market, it would fetch a pretty penny among the fishermen. That he might not lack ready money, she gave him a copper farthing of Birmingham manufacture, being all the coin she had about her, and likewise a great deal of brass, which she applied to his forehead, thus making it yellower than ever.

"With that brass alone," quoth Mother Rigby, "thou canst pay thy way all over the earth. Kiss me, pretty darling! I have done my best for thee."

Furthermore, that the adventurer might lack no possible advantage toward a fair start in life, this excellent old dame gave him a token by which he was to introduce himself to a certain magistrate, member of the council, merchant, and elder of the church (the four capacities constituting but one man), who stood at the head of society in the neighboring metropolis. The token was neither more nor less than a single word, which Mother Rigby whispered to the scarecrow, and which the scarecrow was to whisper to the merchant.

"Gouty as the old fellow is, he'll run thy errands for thee, when once thou hast given him that word in his ear," said the old witch. "Mother Rigby knows the worshipful Justice Gookin, and the worshipful Justice knows Mother Rigby!"

Here the witch thrust her wrinkled face close to the puppet's, chuckling irrepressibly, and fidgeting all through her system, with delight at the idea which she meant to communicate.

"The worshipful Master Gookin," whispered she, "hath a comely maiden to his daughter. And hark ye, my pet! Thou hast a fair outside, and a pretty wit enough of thine own. Yea, a pretty wit enough! Thou wilt think better of it when thou hast seen more of other people's wits. Now, with thy outside and thy inside, thou art the very man to win a young girl's heart. Never doubt it! I tell thee it shall be so. Put but a bold face on the matter, sigh, smile, flourish thy hat, thrust forth thy leg like a dancing master, put thy right hand to the left side of thy waistcoat, and pretty Polly Gookin is thine own!"

All this while the new creature had been sucking in and exhaling the vapory fragrance of his pipe, and seemed now to continue this occupation as much for the enjoyment it afforded as because it was an essential condition of his existence. It was wonderful to see how exceedingly like a human being it behaved. Its eyes (for it appeared to possess a pair) were bent on Mother Rigby, and at suitable junctures it nodded or shook its head. Neither did it lack words proper for the occasion: "Really! Indeed! Pray tell me! Is it possible? Upon my word! By no means! Oh! Ah! Hem!" and other such weighty utterances as imply attention, inquiry, acquiescence, or dissent on the part of the auditor. Even had you stood by and seen the scarecrow made, you could scarcely have resisted the conviction that it perfectly understood the cunning counsels which the old witch poured into its counterfeit of an ear. The more earnestly it applied its lips to the pipe, the more distinctly was its human likeness stamped among visible realities, the more sagacious grew its expression, the more lifelike its gestures and movements, and the more intelligibly audible its voice. Its garments, too, glistened so much the brighter with an illusory magnificence. The very pipe, in which burned the spell of all this wonderwork, ceased to appear as a smoke-blackened earthen stump, and became a meerschaum, with painted bowl and amber mouthpiece.

It might be apprehended, however, that as the life of the illusion seemed identical with the vapor of the pipe, it would terminate simultaneously with the reduction of the tobacco to ashes. But the beldam foresaw the difficulty.

"Hold thou the pipe, my precious one," said she, "While I fill it for thee again."

It was sorrowful to behold how the fine gentleman began to fade back into a scarecrow while Mother Rigby shook the ashes out of the pipe and proceeded to replenish it from her tobacco box.

"Dickon," cried she, in her high, sharp tone, "another coal for this pipe!"

No sooner said than the intensely red speck of fire was glowing within the pipe bowl; and the scarecrow, without waiting for the witch's bidding, applied the tube to his lips and drew in a few short, convulsive whiffs, which soon, however, became regular and equable.

"Now, mine own heart's darling," quoth Mother Rigby, "whatever may happen to thee, thou must stick to thy pipe. Thy life is in it; and that, at least, thou knowest well, if thou knowest nought besides. Stick to thy pipe, I say! Smoke, puff, blow thy cloud; and tell the people, if any question be made, that it is for thy health, and that so the physician orders thee to do. And, sweet one, when thou shalt find thy pipe getting low, go apart into some corner, and (first filling thyself with smoke) cry sharply, 'Dickon, a fresh pipe of tobacco!' and, 'Dickon, another

coal for my pipe!' and have it into thy pretty
mouth as speedily as may be. Else, instead of a
gallant gentleman in a gold-laced coat, thou wilt
be but a jumble of sticks and tattered clothes,
and a bag of straw, and a withered pumpkin!
Now depart, my treasure, and good luck go with
thee!"

"Never fear, mother!" said the figure, in a
stout voice, and sending forth a courageous
whiff of smoke, "I will thrive, if an honest man
and a gentleman may!"

"Oh, thou wilt be the death of me!" cried the
old witch, convulsed with laughter. "That was
well said. If an honest man and a gentleman
may! Thou playest thy part to perfection. Get
along with thee for a smart fellow; and I will
wager on thy head, as a man of pith and substance, with a brain and what they call a heart,
and all else that a man should have, against any
other thing on two legs. I hold myself a better
witch than yesterday, for thy sake. Did not I
make thee? And I defy any witch in New England to make such another! Here; take my staff
along with thee!"

The staff, though it was but a plain oaken
stick, immediately took the aspect of a goldheaded cane.

"That gold head has as much sense in it as
thine own," said Mother Rigby, "and it will
guide thee straight to worshipful Master Gookin's door. Get thee gone, my pretty pet, my
darling, my precious one, my treasure; and if
any ask thy name, it is Feathertop. For thou hast
a feather in thy hat, and I have thrust a hand-

ful of feathers into the hollow of thy head, and
thy wig, too, is of the fashion they call Feathertop — so be Feathertop thy name!"

And, issuing from the cottage, Feathertop
strode manfully toward town. Mother Rigby
stood at the threshold, well pleased to see how
the sunbeams glistened on him, as if all his magnificence were real, and how diligently and lov-
ingly he smoked his pipe, and how handsomely
he walked, in spite of a little stiffness of his legs.
She watched him until out of sight, and threw
a witch benediction after her darling, when a
turn of the road snatched him from her view.

Betimes in the forenoon, when the principal
street of the neighboring town was just at its
acme of life and bustle, a stranger of very distinguished figure was seen on the sidewalk. His
port as well as his garments betokened nothing
short of nobility. He wore a richly embroidered
plum-colored coat, a waistcoat of costly velvet,
magnificently adorned with golden foliage, a
pair of splendid scarlet breeches, and the finest
and glossiest of white silk stockings. His head
was covered with a peruke, so daintily powdered
and adjusted that it would have been sacrilege
to disorder it with a hat; which, therefore (and
it was a goldlaced hat, set off with a snowy
feather), he carried beneath his arm. On the
breast of his coat glistened a star. He managed
his goldheaded cane with an airy grace, peculiar
to the fine gentlemen of the period; and, to give
the highest possible finish to his equipment, he
had lace ruffles at his wrist, of a most ethe-
real delicacy, sufficiently avouching how idle

and aristocratic must be the hands which they half concealed.

It was a remarkable point in the accouterment of this brilliant personage that he held in his left hand a fantastic kind of a pipe, with an exquisitely painted bowl and an amber mouthpiece. This he applied to his lips as often as every five or six paces, and inhaled a deep whiff of smoke, which, after being retained a moment in his lungs, might be seen to eddy gracefully from his mouth and nostrils.

As may well be supposed, the street was all astir to find out the stranger's name.

"It is some great nobleman, beyond question," said one of the townspeople. "Do you see the star at his breast?"

"Nay; it is too bright to be seen," said another. "Yes; he must needs be a nobleman, as you say. But by what conveyance, think you, can his lordship have voyaged or traveled hither? There has been no vessel from the old country for a month past; and if he have arrived overland from the southward, pray where are his attendants and equipage?"

"He needs no equipage to set off his rank," remarked a third. "If he came among us in rags, nobility would shine through a hole in his elbow. I never saw such dignity of aspect. He has the old Norman blood in his veins, I warrant him."

"I rather take him to be a Dutchman, or one of your high Germans," said another citizen. "The men of those countries have always the pipe at their mouths."

"And so has a Turk," answered his companion. "But, in my judgment, this stranger hath been bred at the French court, and hath there learned politeness and grace of manner, which none understand so well as the nobility of France. That gait, now! A vulgar spectator might deem it stiff — he might call it a hitch and jerk — but, to my eye, it hath an unspeakable majesty, and must have been acquired by constant observation of the deportment of the Grand Monarque. The stranger's character and office are evident enough. He is a French ambassador, come to treat with our rulers about the cession of Canada."

"More probably a Spaniard," said another, "and hence his yellow complexion; or, most likely, he is from the Havana, or from some port on the Spanish main, and comes to make investigation about the piracies which our government is thought to connive at. Those settlers in Peru and Mexico have skins as yellow as the gold which they dig out of their mines."

"Yellow or not," cried a lady, "he is a beautiful man! so tall, so slender! Such a fine, noble face, with so well-shaped a nose, and all that delicacy of expression about the mouth! And, bless me, how bright his star is! It positively shoots out flames!"

"So do your eyes, fair lady," said the stranger, with a bow and a flourish of his pipe; for he was just passing at the instant. "Upon my honor, they have quite dazzled me."

"Was ever so original and exquisite a compliment?" murmured the lady, in an ecstasy of delight.

Amid the general admiration excited by the stranger's appearance, there were only two dissenting voices. One was that of an impertinent cur, which, after snuffing at the heels of the glistening figure, put its tail between its legs and skulked into its master's backyard, vociferating an execrable howl. The other dissentient was a young child, who squalled at the fullest stretch of his lungs, and babbled some unintelligible nonsense about a pumpkin.

Feathertop meanwhile pursued his way along the street. Except for the few complimentary words to the lady, and now and then a slight inclination of the head in requital of the profound reverences of the bystanders, he seemed wholly absorbed in his pipe. There needed no other proof of his rank and consequence than the perfect equanimity with which he comported himself, while the curiosity and admiration of the town swelled almost into clamor around him. With a crowd gathering behind his footsteps, he finally reached the mansion-house of the worshipful Justice Gookin, entered the gate, ascended the steps of the front door, and knocked. In the interim, before his summons was answered, the stranger was observed to shake the ashes out of his pipe.

"What did he say in that sharp voice?" inquired one of the spectators.

"Nay, I know not," answered his friend. "But the sun dazzles my eyes strangely. How dim and faded his lordship looks all of a sudden!

Bless my wits, what is the matter with me?"

"The wonder is," said the other, "that his pipe, which was out only an instant ago, should be all alight again, and with the reddest coal I ever saw. There is something mysterious about this stranger. What a whiff of smoke was that! Dim and faded did you call him? Why, as he turns about the star on his breast is all ablaze."

"It is, indeed," said his companion; "and it will go near to dazzle pretty Polly Gookin, whom I see peeping at it out of the chamber window."

The door being now opened, Feathertop turned to the crowd, made a stately bend of his body like a great man acknowledging the reverence of the meaner sort, and vanished into the house. There was a mysterious kind of a smile, if it might not better be called a grin or grimace, upon his visage; but, of all the throng that beheld him, not an individual appears to have possessed insight enough to detect the illusive character of the stranger except a little child and a cur dog.

Our legend here loses somewhat of its continuity, and, passing over the preliminary explanation between Feathertop and the merchant, goes in quest of the pretty Polly Gookin. She was a damsel of a soft, round figure, with light hair and blue eyes, and a fair, rosy face, which seemed neither very shrewd nor very simple. This young lady had caught a glimpse of the glistening stranger while standing on the threshold, and had forthwith put on a laced cap, a string of beads, her finest kerchief, and her stiffest damask petticoat in preparation for the interview. Hurrying from her chamber to the parlor, she had ever since been viewing herself in the large looking glass and practicing pretty airs — now a smile, now a ceremonious dignity of aspect, and now a softer smile than the former, kissing her hand likewise, tossing her head, and managing her fan; while within the mirror an unsubstantial little maid repeated every gesture and did all the foolish things that Polly did, but without making her ashamed of them. In short, it was the fault of pretty Polly's ability rather than her will if she failed to be as complete an artifice as the illustrious Feathertop himself; and, when she thus tampered with her own simplicity, the witch's phantom might well hope to win her.

No sooner did Polly hear her father's gouty footsteps approaching the parlor door, accompanied with the stiff clatter of Feathertop's highheeled shoes, then she seated herself bolt upright and innocently began warbling a song.

"Polly! daughter Polly!" cried the old merchant. "Come hither, child."

Master Gookin's aspect, as he opened the door, was doubtful and troubled.

"This gentleman," continued he, presenting the stranger, "is the Chevalier Feathertop — nay, I beg his pardon, my Lord Feathertop — who hath brought me a token of remembrance from an ancient friend of mine. Pay your duty to his lordship, child, and honor him as his quality deserves."

After these few words of introduction, the

worshipful magistrate immediately quitted the room. But, even in that brief moment, had the fair Polly glanced aside at her father instead of devoting herself wholly to the brilliant guest, she might have taken warning of some mischief nigh at hand. The old man was nervous, fidgety, and very pale. Purposing a smile of courtesy, he had deformed his face with a sort of galvanic grin, which, when Feathertop's back was turned, he exchanged for a scowl, at the same time shaking his fist and stamping his gouty foot — an incivility which brought its retribution along with it. The truth appears to have been that Mother Rigby's word of introduction, whatever it might be, had operated far more on the rich merchant's fears than on his good will. Moreover, being a man of wonderfully acute observation, he had noticed that these painted figures on the bowl of Feathertop's pipe were in motion. Looking more closely, he became convinced that these figures were a party of little demons, each duly provided with horns and a tail, and dancing hand in hand, with gestures of diabolical merriment, round the circumference of the pipe bowl. As if to confirm his suspicions, while Master Gookin ushered his guest along a dusky passage from his private room to the parlor, the star on Feathertop's breast had scintillated actual flames, and threw a flickering gleam upon the wall, the ceiling, and the floor.

With such sinister prognostics manifesting themselves on all hands, it is not to be marveled at that the merchant should have felt that he was committing his daughter to a very questionable acquaintance. He cursed, in his secret soul, the insinuating elegance of Feathertop's manners, as this brilliant personage bowed, smiled, put his hand on his heart, inhaled a long whiff from his pipe, and enriched the atmosphere with the smoky vapor of a fragrant and visible sigh. Gladly would poor Master Gookin have thrust his dangerous guest into the street; but there was a constraint and terror within him. This respectable old gentleman, we fear, at an earlier period of life, had given some pledge or other to the evil principle, and perhaps was now to redeem it by the sacrifice of his daughter.

It so happened that the parlor door was partly of glass, shaded by a silken curtain, the folds of which hung a little awry. So strong was the merchant's interest in witnessing what was to ensue between the fair Polly and the gallant Feathertop that, after quitting the room, he could by no means refrain from peeping through the crevice of the curtain.

But there was nothing very miraculous to be seen; nothing — except the trifles previously noticed — to confirm the idea of a supernatural peril environing the pretty Polly. The stranger it is true was evidently a thorough and practiced man of the world, systematic and self-possessed, and therefore the sort of a person to whom a parent ought not to confide a simple, young girl without due watchfulness for the result. The worthy magistrate, who had been conversant with all degrees and qualities of mankind, could not but perceive every motion and gesture of the distinguished Feathertop came in its proper place; nothing had been left rude or native in him; a well-digested conventionalism had incorporated itself thoroughly with his substance and transformed him into a work of art. Perhaps it was this peculiarity that invested him with a species of ghastliness and awe. It is the effect of anything completely and consummately artificial, in human shape, that the person impresses us as an unreality and as having hardly pith enough to cast a shadow upon the floor. As regarded Feathertop, all this resulted in a wild, extravagant, and fantastical impression, as if his life and being were akin to the smoke that curled upward from his pipe.

But pretty Polly Gookin felt not thus. The pair were now promenading the room: Feathertop with his dainty stride and no less dainty grimace: the girl with a native maidenly grace, just touched, not spoiled, by a slightly affected manner, which seemed caught from the perfect artifice of her companion. The longer the interview continued, the more charmed was pretty Polly, until, within the first quarter of an hour (as the old magistrate noted by his watch), she was evidently beginning to be in love. Nor need it have been witchcraft that subdued her in such a hurry; the poor child's heart, it may be, was so very fervent that it melted her with its own warmth as reflected from the hollow semblance of a lover. No matter what Feathertop said, his words found depth and reverberation in her ear; no matter what he did, his action was heroic to her eye. And by this time it is to be supposed there was a blush on Polly's cheek, a tender smile about her mouth, and a liquid softness in her glance; while the star kept coruscating on Feathertop's breast, and the little demons careered with more frantic merriment than ever about the circumference of his pipe bowl. O pretty Polly Gookin, why should these imps rejoice so madly that a silly maiden's heart was about to be given to a shadow! Is it so unusual a misfortune, so rare a triumph?

By and by Feathertop paused, and throwing himself into an imposing attitude, seemed to summon the fair girl to survey his figure and resist him longer if she could. His star, his embroidery, his buckles glowed at that instant with unutterable splendor; the picturesque hues of his attire took a richer depth of coloring; there was a gleam and polish over his whole presence betokening the perfect witchery of well-ordered manners. The maiden raised her eyes and suffered them to linger upon her companion with a bashful and admiring gaze. Then, as if desirous of judging what value her own simple comeliness might have side by side with so much brilliancy, she cast a glance toward the full-length looking glass in front of which they happened to be standing. It was one of the truest plates in the world and incapable of flattery. No sooner did the images therein reflected meet Polly's eye than she shrieked, shrank from the stranger's side, gazed at him for a moment in the wildest dismay, and sank insensible upon the floor. Feathertop likewise had looked toward the mirror, and there beheld, not the glittering mockery of his outside show, but a picture of the sordid patchwork of his real composition, stripped of all witchcraft.

The wretched simulacrum! We almost pity him. He threw up his arms with an expression of despair that went further than any of his previous manifestations toward vindicating his claims to be reckoned human; for, perchance the only time since this so often empty and deceptive life of mortals began its course, an illusion had seen and fully recognized itself.

Mother Rigby was seated by her kitchen hearth in the twilight of this eventful day, and had just shaken the ashes out of a new pipe, when she heard a hurried tramp along the road. Yet it did not seem so much the tramp of human footsteps as the clatter of sticks or the rattling of dry bones.

"Ha!" thought the old witch, "what step is that? Whose skeleton is out of its grave now, I wonder?"

A figure burst headlong into the cottage door. It was Feathertop! His pipe was still alight; the star still flamed upon his breast; the embroidery still glowed upon his garments; nor had he lost, in any degree or manner that could be estimated, the aspect that assimilated him with our mortal brotherhood. But yet, in some indescribable way (as is the case with all that has deluded us when once found out), the poor reality was felt beneath the cunning artifice.

"What has gone wrong?" demanded the witch. "Did yonder sniffling hypocrite thrust my darling from his door? The villain! I'll set twenty fiends to torment him till he offer thee his daughter on his bended knees!"

"No, mother," said Feathertop despondingly; "it was not that."

"Did the girl scorn my precious one?" asked Mother Rigby, her fierce eyes glowing like two coals of Tophet. "I'll cover her face with pimples! Her nose shall be as red as the coal in thy pipe! Her front teeth shall drop out! In a week hence she shall not be worth thy having!"

"Let her alone, mother," answered poor Feathertop; "the girl was half won; and methinks a kiss from her sweet lips might have made me altogether human. But," he added, after a brief pause and then a howl of self-contempt, "I've seen myself, mother! I've seen myself for the wretched, ragged, empty thing I am! I'll exist no longer!"

Snatching the pipe from his mouth, he flung it with all his might against the chimney, and at the same instant sank upon the floor, a medley of straw and tattered garments, with some sticks protruding from the heap, and a shriveled pumpkin in the midst. The eyeholes were now lusterless; but the rudely carved gap, that just before had been a mouth, still seemed to twist itself into a despairing grin, and was so far human.

"Poor fellow!" quoth Mother Rigby, with a rueful glance at the relics of her ill-fated contrivance. "My poor, dear, pretty Feathertop! There are thousands upon thousands of coxcombs and charlatans in the world, made up of just a jumble of wornout, forgotten, and good-for-nothing trash as he was! Yet they live in fair repute, and never see themselves for what they are. And why should my poor puppet be the only one to know himself and perish for it?"

While thus muttering, the witch had filled a fresh pipe of tobacco, and held the stem between her fingers, as doubtful whether to thrust it into her own mouth or Feathertop's.

"Poor Feathertop!" she continued. "I could easily give him another chance and send him forth again tomorrow. But no; his feelings are too tender, his sensibilities too deep. He seems to have too much heart to bustle for his own advantage in such an empty and heartless world. Well! well! I'll make a scarecrow of him after all. 'Tis an innocent and useful vocation, and will suit my darling well; and, if each of his human brethren had as fit a one, 't would be the better for mankind; and as for this pipe of tobacco, I need it more than he."

So saying, Mother Rigby put the stem between her lips. "Dickon!" cried she, in her high, sharp tone, "another coal for my pipe!"

WAKEFIELD

IN SOME OLD MAGAZINE or newspaper I recollect
a story, told as truth, of a man—let us call him
Wakefield—who absented himself for a long time
from his wife. The fact, thus abstractedly stated,
is not very uncommon, nor—without a proper
distinction of circumstances—to be condemned
either as naughty or nonsensical. Howbeit, this,
though far from the most aggravated, is perhaps
the strangest instance on record, of marital de-
linquency; and, moreover, as remarkable a freak
as may be found in the whole list of human
oddities. The wedded couple lived in London.
The man, under pretence of going on a journey,
took lodgings in the next street to his own house,
and there, unheard of by his wife or friends, and
without the shadow of a reason for such self-ban-
ishment, dwelt upward of twenty years. During

that period, he beheld his home every day, and frequently the forlorn Mrs. Wakefield. And after so great a gap in his matrimonial felicity—when his death was reckoned certain, his estate settled, his name dismissed from memory, and his wife, long, long ago, resigned to her autumnal widowhood—he entered the door one evening, quietly, as from a day's absence, and became a loving spouse till death.

This outline is all that I remember. But the incident, though of the purest originality, unexampled, and probably never to be repeated, is one, I think, which appeals to the generous sympathies of mankind. We know, each for himself, that none of us would perpetrate such a folly, yet feel as if some other might. To my own contemplations, at least, it has often recurred, always exciting wonder, but with a sense that the story must be true, and a conception of its hero's character. Whenever any subject so forcibly affects the mind, time is well spent in thinking of it. If the reader choose, let him do his own meditation; or if he prefer to ramble with me through the twenty years of Wakefield's vagary, I bid him welcome; trusting that there will be a pervading spirit and a moral, even should we fail to find them, done up neatly, and condensed into the final sentence. Thought has always its efficacy, and every striking incident its moral.

What sort of a man was Wakefield? We are free to shape out our own idea, and call it by his name. He was now in the meridian of life; his matrimonial affections, never violent, were

sobered into a calm, habitual sentiment; of all
husbands, he was likely to be the most constant,
because a certain sluggishness would keep his
heart at rest, wherever it might be placed. He
was intellectual, but not actively so; his mind
occupied itself in long and lazy musings, that
ended to no purpose, or had not vigor to attain
it; his thoughts were seldom so energetic as to
seize hold of words. Imagination, in the proper
meaning of the term, made no part of Wakefield's gifts. With a cold but not depraved nor
wandering heart, and a mind never feverish
with riotous thoughts, nor perplexed with originality, who could have anticipated that our
friend would entitle himself to a foremost place
among the doers of eccentric deeds? Had his acquaintances been asked, who was the man in
London the surest to perform nothing today
which should be remembered on the morrow,
they would have thought of Wakefield. Only the
wife of his bosom might have hesitated. She,
without having analyzed his character, was
partly aware of a quiet selfishness, that had
rusted into his inactive mind; of a peculiar sort
of vanity, the most uneasy attribute about him;
of a disposition to craft which had seldom produced more positive effects than the keeping of
petty secrets, hardly worth revealing; and, lastly,
of what she called a little strangeness, sometimes,
in the good man. This latter quality is indefinable, and perhaps nonexistent.

Let us now imagine Wakefield bidding adieu
to his wife. It is the dusk of an October evening.
His equipment is a drab greatcoat, a hat covered

with an oilcloth, top boots, an umbrella in one hand and a small portmanteau in the other. He has informed Mrs. Wakefield that he is to take the night coach into the country. She would fain inquire the length of his journey, its object, and the probable time of his return; but, indulgent to his harmless love of mystery, interrogates him only by a look. He tells her not to expect him positively by the return coach, nor to be alarmed should he tarry three or four days; but, at all events, to look for him at supper on Friday evening. Wakefield himself, be it considered, has no suspicion of what is before him. He holds out his hand, she gives her own, and meets his part- ing kiss in the matter-of-course way of a ten years' matrimony; and forth goes the middle- aged Mr. Wakefield, almost resolved to per- plex his good lady by a whole week's absence. After the door has closed behind him, she per- ceives it thrust partly open, and a vision of her husband's face, through the aperture, smiling on her, and gone in a moment. For the time, this little incident is dismissed without a thought. But, long afterward, when she has been more years a widow than a wife, that smile recurs, and flickers across all her reminiscences of Wake- field's visage. In her many musings, she sur- rounds the original smile with a multitude of fantasies, which make it strange and awful: as, for instance, if she imagines him in a coffin, that parting look is frozen on his pale features; or, if she dreams of him in heaven, still his blessed spirit wears a quiet and crafty smile. Yet, for its sake, when all others have given him up for dead, she sometimes doubts whether she is a widow.

But our business is with the husband. We must hurry after him along the street, ere he lose his individuality, and melt into the great mass of London life. It would be vain searching for him there. Let us follow close at his heels, therefore, until, after several superfluous turns and doublings, we find him comfortably established by the fireside of a small apartment, previously bespoken. He is in the next street to his own, and at his journey's end. He can scarcely trust his good fortune, in having got thither unperceived — recollecting that, at one time, he was delayed by the throng, in the very focus of a lighted lantern; and, again, there were footsteps that seemed to tread behind his own, distinct from the multitudinous tramp around him; and, anon, he heard a voice shouting afar, and fancied that it called his name. Doubtless, a dozen busybodies had been watching him, and told his wife the whole affair. Poor Wakefield! Little knowest thou thine own insignificance in this great world! No mortal eye but mine has traced thee. Go quietly to thy bed, foolish man; and, on the morrow, if thou wilt be wise, get thee home to good Mrs. Wakefield, and tell her the truth. Remove not thyself, even for a little week, from thy place in her chaste bosom. Were she, for a single moment, to deem thee dead, or lost, or lastingly divided from her, thou wouldst be woefully conscious of a change in thy true wife forever after. It is perilous to make a chasm in human affections; not that they gape so long and wide — but so quickly close again!

Almost repenting of his frolic, or whatever it may be termed, Wakefield lies down betimes, and starting from his first nap, spreads forth his arms into the wide and solitary waste of the unaccustomed bed. "No," thinks he, gathering the bedclothes about him, "I will not sleep alone another night."

In the morning he rises earlier than usual, and sets himself to consider what he really means to do. Such are his loose and rambling modes of thought that he has taken this very singular step with the consciousness of a purpose, indeed, but without being able to define it sufficiently for his own contemplation. The vagueness of the project, and the convulsive effort with which he plunges into the execution of it, are equally characteristic of a feebleminded man. Wakefield sifts his ideas, however, as minutely as he may, and finds himself curious to know the progress of matters at home — how his exemplary wife will endure her widowhood of a week; and, briefly, how the little sphere of creatures and circumstances, in which he was a central object, will be affected by his removal. A morbid vanity, therefore, lies nearest the bottom of the affair. But, how is he to attain his ends? Not, certainly, by keeping close in this comfortable lodging, where, though he slept and awoke in the next street to his home, he is as effectually abroad as if the stagecoach had been whirling him away all night. Yet, should he reappear, the whole project is knocked in the head. His poor brains being hopelessly puzzled with this dilemma, he at length ventures out, partly resolving to cross the head of the street, and send one hasty glance toward his forsaken domicile. Habit — for he is a man of habits — takes him by the hand, and guides him, wholly unaware, to his own door, where, just at the critical moment, he is aroused by the scraping of his foot upon the step. Wakefield! whither are you going?

At that instant his fate was turning on the pivot. Little dreaming of the doom to which his first backward step devotes him, he hurries away, breathless with agitation hitherto unfelt, and hardly dares turn his head at the distant corner. Can it be that nobody caught sight of him? Will not the whole household — the decent Mrs. Wakefield, the smart maid servant, and the dirty little footboy — raise a hue and cry, through London streets, in pursuit of their fugitive lord and master? Wonderful escape! He gathers courage to pause and look homeward, but is perplexed with a sense of change about the familiar edifice, such as affects us all, when, after a separation of months or years, we again see some hill or lake, or work of art, with which we were friends of old. In ordinary cases, this indescribable impression is caused by the comparison and contrast between our imperfect reminiscences and the reality. In Wakefield, the magic of a single night has wrought a similar transformation, because, in that brief period, a great moral change has been effected. But this is a secret from himself. Before leaving the spot, he catches a far and momentary glimpse of his wife, passing athwart the front window, with her face turned toward the head of the street. The crafty nincompoop takes to his heels, scared with the idea that, among a thousand such atoms of mortality, her eye must have detected him. Right glad is his heart, though his brain be somewhat dizzy, when he finds himself by the coal fire of his lodgings.

So much for the commencement of this long whimwham. After the initial conception, and the stirring up of the man's sluggish temperament to put it in practice, the whole matter evolves itself in a natural train. We may suppose him, as the result of deep deliberation, buying a new wig, of reddish hair, and selecting sundry garments, in a fashion unlike his customary suit of brown, from a Jew's old-clothes bag. It is accomplished. Wakefield is another man. The new system being now established, a retrograde movement to the old would be almost as difficult as the step that placed him in his unparalleled position. Furthermore, he is rendered obstinate by a sulkiness occasionally incident to his temper, and brought on at present by the inadequate sensation which he conceives to have been produced in the bosom of Mrs. Wakefield. He will not go back until she be frightened half to death. Well; twice or thrice has she passed before his sight, each time with a heavier step, a paler cheek, and more anxious brow; and in the third week of his nonappearance he detects a portent of evil entering the house, in the guise of an apothecary. Next day the knocker is muffled. Toward nightfall comes the chariot of a physician, and deposits its big-wigged and solemn burden at Wakefield's door, whence, after a quarter of an hour's visit, he emerges, perchance the herald of a funeral. Dear woman! Will she die? By this time, Wakefield is excited to something like energy of feeling, but still lingers away from his wife's bedside, pleading with his conscience that she must not be disturbed at such a juncture. If aught else restrains him, he does not know it. In the course of a few weeks she gradually recovers; the crisis is over; her heart is sad, perhaps, but quiet; and, let him return soon or late, it will never be feverish for him again. Such ideas glimmer through the midst of Wakefield's mind, and render him indistinctly conscious that an almost impassable gulf divides his hired apartment from his former home. "It is but in the next street!" he sometimes says. Fool! it is in another world. Hitherto, he has put off his return from one particular day to another; henceforward, he leaves the precise time undetermined. Not tomorrow — probably next week — pretty soon. Poor man! The dead have nearly as much chance of revisiting their earthly homes as the selfbanished Wakefield.

Would that I had a folio to write, instead of an article of a dozen pages! Then might I exemplify how an influence beyond our control lays its strong hand on every deed which we do, and weaves its consequences into an iron tissue of necessity. Wakefield is spellbound. We must leave him, for ten years or so, to haunt around his house, without once crossing the threshold, and to be faithful to his wife, with all the affection of which his heart is capable, while he is slowly fading out of hers. Long since, it must be remarked, he had lost the perception of singularity in his conduct.

Now for a scene! Among the throng of a London street we distinguish a man, now waxing elderly, with few characteristics to attract careless observers, yet bearing, in his whole aspect, the handwriting of no common fate, for such as have the skill to read it. He is meager; his low and narrow forehead is deeply wrinkled; his eyes, small and lusterless, sometimes wander apprehensively about him, but oftener seem to look inward. He bends his head, and moves with an indescribable obliquity of gait, as if unwilling to display his full front to the world. Watch him long enough to see what we have described, and you will allow that circumstances — which often produce remarkable men from nature's ordinary handiwork — have produced one such here. Next, leaving him to sidle along the footwalk, cast your eyes in the opposite direction, where a portly female, considerably in the wane of life, with a prayerbook in her hand, is proceeding to yonder church. She has the placid mien of settled widowhood. Her regrets have either died away, or have become so essential to her heart, that they would be poorly exchanged for joy. Just as the lean man and well-conditioned woman are passing, a slight obstruction occurs, and brings these two figures directly in contact. Their hands touch; the pressure of the crowd forces her bosom against his shoulder; they stand, face to face, staring into each other's eyes. After a ten years' separation, thus Wakefield meets his wife!

The throng eddies away, and carries them asunder. The sober widow, resuming her former pace, proceeds to church, but pauses in the portal, and throws a perplexed glance along the street. She passes in, however, opening her prayerbook as she goes. And the man! With so wild a face that busy and selfish London stands to gaze after him, he hurries to his lodgings, bolts the door, and throws himself upon the bed. The latent feelings of years break out; his feeble mind acquires a brief energy from their strength; all the miserable strangeness of his life is revealed to him at a glance: and he cries out, passionately, "Wakefield! Wakefield! You are mad!"

Perhaps he was so. The singularity of his situation must have so molded him to himself, that, considered in regard to his fellow creatures and the business of life, he could not be said to possess his right mind. He had contrived, or rather he had happened, to dissever himself from the world — to vanish — to give up his place and privileges with living men, without being admitted among the dead. The life of a hermit is nowise parallel to his. He was in the bustle of the city, as of old; but the crowd swept by and saw him not; he was, we may figuratively say, always beside his wife and at his hearth, yet must never feel the warmth of the one nor the affection of the other. It was Wakefield's unprecedented fate to retain his original share of human sympathies, and to be still involved in human interests, while he had lost his reciprocal influence on them. It would be a most curious speculation to trace out the effect of such circumstances on his heart and intellect, separately, and in unison. Yet, changed as he was, he would seldom be conscious of it, but deem himself the same man as ever; glimpses of the truth, indeed, would come, but only for the moment; and still he would keep saying, "I shall soon go back!" — nor reflect that he had been saying so for twenty years.

I conceive, also, that these twenty years would appear, in the retrospect, scarcely longer than the week to which Wakefield had at first limited his absence. He would look on the affair as no more than an interlude in the main business of his life. When, after a little while more, he should deem it time to re-enter his parlor, his wife would clap her hands for joy, on beholding the middle-aged Mr. Wakefield. Alas, what a mistake! Would Time but await the close of our favorite follies, we should be young men, all of us, and till Doomsday.

One evening, in the twentieth year since he vanished, Wakefield is taking his customary walk toward the dwelling which he still calls his own. It is a gusty night of autumn, with frequent showers that patter down upon the pavement, and are gone before a man can put up his umbrella. Pausing near the house, Wakefield discerns, through the parlor windows of the second floor, the red glow and the glimmer and fitful flash of a comfortable fire. On the ceiling appears a grotesque shadow of good Mrs. Wakefield. The cap, the nose and chin, and the broad waist, form an admirable caricature, which dances, moreover, with the up-flickering and

down-sinking blaze, almost too merrily for the
shade of an elderly widow. At this instant a
shower chances to fall, and is driven, by the un-
mannerly gust, full into Wakefield's face and
bosom. He is quite penetrated with its autumnal
chill. Shall he stand, wet and shivering here,
when his own hearth has a good fire to warm
him, and his own wife will run to fetch the gray
coat and small-clothes, which, doubtless, she
has kept carefully in the closet of their bed chamber? No! Wakefield is no such fool. He ascends
the steps — heavily! — for twenty years have
stiffened his legs since he came down — but he
knows it not. Stay, Wakefield! Would you go to
the sole home that is left you? Then step into
your grave! The door opens. As he passes in, we
have a parting glimpse of his visage, and recognize the crafty smile, which was the precursor of
the little joke that he has ever since been playing off at his wife's expense. How unmercifully
has he quizzed the poor woman! Well, a good
night's rest to Wakefield!

This happy event — supposing it to be such
— could only have occurred at an unpremedi-
tated moment. We will not follow our friend
across the threshold. He has left us much food
for thought, a portion of which shall lend its
wisdom to a moral, and be shaped into a figure.
Amid the seeming confusion of our mysterious
world, individuals are so nicely adjusted to a
system, and systems to one another and to a
whole, that, by stepping aside for a moment, a
man exposes himself to a fearful risk of losing
his place forever. Like Wakefield, he may become, as it were, the Outcast of the Universe.

THE AMBITIOUS GUEST

ONE SEPTEMBER NIGHT a family had gathered round their hearth, and piled it high with the driftwood of mountain streams, the dry cones of the pine, and the splintered ruins of great trees that had come crashing down the precipice. Up the chimney roared the fire, and brightened the room with its broad blaze. The faces of the father and mother had a sober gladness; the children laughed; the eldest daughter was the image of Happiness at seventeen; and the aged grandmother, who sat knitting in the warmest place, was the image of Happiness grown old. They had found the "herb, heart's-ease," in the bleakest spot of all New England. This family were situated in the Notch of the White Hills, where the wind was sharp throughout the year, and pitilessly cold in the winter —

giving their cottage all its fresh inclemency before it descended on the valley of the Saco. They
dwelt in a cold spot and a dangerous one; for a
mountain towered above their heads, so steep,
that the stones would often rumble down its sides
and startle them at midnight.

The daughter had just uttered some simple
jest that filled them all with mirth, when the
wind came through the Notch and seemed to
pause before their cottage — rattling the door,
with a sound of wailing and lamentation, before
it passed into the valley. For a moment it saddened them, though there was nothing unusual
in the tones. But the family were glad again
when they perceived that the latch was lifted by
some traveler, whose footsteps had been unheard
amid the dreary blast which heralded his approach, and wailed as he was entering, and went
moaning away from the door.

Though they dwelt in such a solitude, these
people held daily converse with the world. The
romantic pass of the Notch is a great artery,
through which the lifeblood of internal commerce is continually throbbing between Maine,
on one side, and the Green Mountains and the
shores of the St. Lawrence, on the other. The
stagecoach always drew up before the door of
the cottage. The wayfarer, with no companion
but his staff, paused here to exchange a word,
that the sense of loneliness might not utterly
overcome him ere he could pass through the
cleft of the mountain, or reach the first house in
the valley. And here the teamster, on his way to
Portland market, would put up for the night;

and, if a bachelor, might sit an hour beyond the usual bedtime, and steal a kiss from the mountain maid at parting. It was one of those primitive taverns where the traveler pays only for food and lodging, but meets with a homely kindness beyond all price. When the footsteps were heard, therefore, between the outer door and the inner one, the whole family rose up, grandmother, children, and all, as if about to welcome someone who belonged to them, and whose fate was linked with theirs.

The door was opened by a young man. His face at first wore the melancholy expression, almost despondency, of one who travels a wild and bleak road, at nightfall and alone, but soon brightened up when he saw the kindly warmth of his reception. He felt his heart spring forward to meet them all, from the old woman, who wiped a chair with her apron, to the little child that held out its arms to him. One glance and smile placed the stranger on a footing of innocent familiarity with the eldest daughter.

"Ah, this fire is the right thing!" cried he; "especially when there is such a pleasant circle round it. I am quite benumbed; for the Notch is just like the pipe of a great pair of bellows; it has blown a terrible blast in my face all the way from Bartlett."

"Then you are going toward Vermont?" said the master of the house, as he helped to take a light knapsack off the young man's shoulders.

"Yes; to Burlington, and far enough beyond," replied he. "I meant to have been at Ethan Crawford's tonight; but a pedestrian lingers along such a road as this. It is no matter; for, when I saw this good fire, and all your cheerful faces, I felt as if you had kindled it on purpose for me, and were waiting my arrival. So I shall sit down among you, and make myself at home."

The frank-hearted stranger had just drawn his chair to the fire when something like a heavy footstep was heard without, rushing down the steep side of the mountain, as with long and rapid strides, and taking such a leap in passing the cottage as to strike the opposite precipice. The family held their breath, because they knew the sound, and their guest held his by instinct.

"The old mountain has thrown a stone at us, for fear we should forget him," said the landlord, recovering himself. "He sometimes nods his head and threatens to come down; but we are old neighbors, and agree together pretty well upon the whole. Besides we have a sure place of refuge hard by if he should be coming in good earnest."

Let us now suppose the stranger to have finished his supper of bear's meat; and, by his natural felicity of manner, to have placed himself on a footing of kindness with the whole family, so that they talked as freely together as if he belonged to their mountain brood. He was of a proud, yet gentle spirit — haughty and reserved among the rich and great; but ever ready to stoop his head to the lowly cottage door, and be like a brother or a son at the poor man's fireside. In the household of the Notch he found warmth and simplicity of feeling, the pervading intelligence of New England, and a poetry

of native growth, which they had gathered when
they little thought of it from the mountain peaks
and chasms, and at the very threshold of their
romantic and dangerous abode. He had traveled
far and alone; his whole life, indeed, had been a
solitary path; for, with the lofty caution of his
nature, he had kept himself apart from those
who might otherwise have been his companions.
The family, too, though so kind and hospitable,
had that consciousness of unity among themselves, and separation from the world at large,
which, in every domestic circle, should still keep
a holy place where no stranger may intrude. But
this evening a prophetic sympathy impelled the
refined and educated youth to pour out his heart
before the simple mountaineers, and con-
strained them to answer him with the same free
confidence. And thus it should have been. Is not
the kindred of a common fate a closer tie than
that of birth?

The secret of the young man's character was
a high and abstracted ambition. He could have
borne to live an undistinguished life, but not
to be forgotten in the grave. Yearning desire
had been transformed to hope; and hope, long
cherished, had become like certainty, that, obscurely as he journeyed now, a glory was to beam
on all his pathway — though not, perhaps, while
he was treading it. But when posterity should
gaze back into the gloom of what was now the
present, they would trace the brightness of his
footsteps, brightening as meaner glories faded,
and confess that a gifted one had passed from

his cradle to his tomb with none to recognize him.

"As yet," cried the stranger — his cheek glowing and his eye flashing with enthusiasm — "as yet, I have done nothing. Were I to vanish from the earth tomorrow, none would know so much of me as you: that a nameless youth came up at nightfall from the valley of the Saco, and opened his heart to you in the evening, and passed through the Notch by sunrise, and was seen no more. Not a soul would ask, 'Who was he? Whither did the wanderer go?' But I cannot die till I have achieved my destiny. Then, let Death come! I shall have built my monument!"

There was a continual flow of natural emotion, gushing forth amid abstracted reverie, which enabled the family to understand this young man's sentiments, though so foreign from their own. With quick sensibility of the ludicrous, he blushed at the ardor into which he had been betrayed.

"You laugh at me," said he, taking the eldest daughter's hand, and laughing himself. "You think my ambition as nonsensical as if I were to freeze myself to death on the top of Mount Washington, only that people might spy at me from the country round about. And, truly, that would be a noble pedestal for a man's statue!"

"It is better to sit here by this fire," answered the girl, blushing, "and be comfortable and contented, though nobody thinks about us."

"I suppose," said her father, after a fit of musing, "there is something natural in what the young man says; and if my mind had been turned that way, I might have felt just the same. It is strange, wife, how his talk has set my head running on things that are pretty certain never to come to pass."

"Perhaps they may," observed the wife. "Is the man thinking what he will do when he is a widower?"

"No, no!" cried he, repelling the idea with reproachful kindness. "When I think of your death, Esther, I think of mine, too. But I was wishing we had a good farm in Bartlett, or Bethlehem, or Littleton, or some other township round the White Mountains; but not where they could tumble on our heads. I should want to stand well with my neighbors and be called Squire, and sent to General Court for a term or two; for a plain, honest man may do as much good there as a lawyer. And when I should be grown quite an old man, and you an old woman, so as not to be long apart, I might die happy enough in my bed, and leave you all crying around me. A slate gravestone would suit me as well as a marble one — with just my name and age, and a verse of a hymn, and something to let people know that I lived an honest man and died a Christian."

"There now!" exclaimed the stranger; "it is our nature to desire a monument, be it slate or marble, or a pillar of granite, or a glorious memory in the universal heart of man."

"We're in a strange way, tonight," said the wife, with tears in her eyes. "They say it's a sign of something, when folks' minds go a wandering so. Hark to the children!"

They listened accordingly. The younger children had been put to bed in another room, but with an open door between, so that they could be heard talking busily among themselves. One and all seemed to have caught the infection from the fireside circle, and were outvying each other in wild wishes, and childish projects of what they would do when they came to be men and women. At length a little boy, instead of addressing his brothers and sisters, called out to his mother.

"I'll tell you what I wish, mother," cried he. "I want you and father and grandma'm, and all of us, and the stranger too, to start right away, and go and take a drink out of the basin of the Flume!"

Nobody could help laughing at the child's notion of leaving a warm bed, and dragging them from a cheerful fire, to visit the basin of the Flume — a brook, which tumbles over the precipice, deep within the Notch. The boy had hardly spoken when a wagon rattled along the road, and stopped a moment before the door. It appeared to contain two or three men, who were cheering their hearts with the rough chorus of a song, which resounded, in broken notes, between the cliffs, while the singers hesitated whether to continue their journey or put up here for the night.

"Father," said the girl, "they are calling you by name."

But the good man doubted whether they had really called him, and was unwilling to show himself too solicitous of gain by inviting people to patronize his house. He therefore did not hurry to the door; and the lash being soon applied, the travelers plunged into the Notch, still singing and laughing, though their music and mirth came back drearily from the heart of the mountain.

"There, mother!" cried the boy, again. "They'd have given us a ride to the Flume."

Again they laughed at the child's pertinacious fancy for a night ramble. But it happened that a light cloud passed over the daughter's spirit; she looked gravely into the fire, and drew a breath that was almost a sigh. It forced its way, in spite of a little struggle to repress it. Then starting and blushing, she looked quickly round the circle, as if they had caught a glimpse into her bosom. The stranger asked what she had been thinking of.

"Nothing," answered she, with a downcast smile. "Only I felt lonesome just then."

"Oh, I have always had a gift of feeling what is in other people's hearts," said he, half seriously. "Shall I tell the secrets of yours? For I know what to think when a young girl shivers by a warm hearth, and complains of lonesomeness at her mother's side. Shall I put these feelings into words?"

"They would not be a girl's feelings any longer if they could be put into words," replied the mountain nymph, laughing, but avoiding his eye.

All this was said apart. Perhaps a germ of love was springing in their hearts, so pure that it might blossom in Paradise, since it could not be matured on earth; for women worship such gentle dignity as his; and the proud, contemplative, yet kindly soul is oftenest captivated by simplicity like hers. But while they spoke softly, and he was watching the happy sadness, the lightsome shadows, the shy yearnings of a maiden's nature, the wind through the Notch took a deeper and drearier sound. It seemed, as the fanciful stranger said, like the choral strain of the spirits of the blast, who in old Indian times had their dwelling among these mountains, and made their heights and recesses a sacred region. There was a wail along the road, as if a funeral were passing. To chase away the gloom, the family threw pine branches on their fire, till the dry leaves crackled and the flame arose, discovering once again a scene of peace and humble happiness. The light hovered about them fondly, and caressed them all. There were the little faces of the children, peeping from their bed apart, and here the father's frame of strength, the mother's subdued and careful mien, the high-browed youth, the budding girl, and the good old grandam, still knitting in the warmest place. The aged woman looked up from her task, and, with fingers ever busy, was the next to speak.

"Old folks have their notions," said she, "as well as young ones. You've been wishing and planning; and letting your heads run on one thing and another, till you've set my mind a wandering too. Now what should an old woman wish for, when she can go but a step or two before she comes to her grave? Children, it will haunt me night and day till I tell you."

"What is it, mother?" cried the husband and wife at once.

Then the old woman, with an air of mystery which drew the circle closer round the fire, informed them that she had provided her grave-clothes some years before — a nice linen shroud, a cap with a muslin ruff, and everything of a finer sort than she had worn since her wedding day. But this evening an old superstition had strangely recurred to her. It used to be said, in her younger days, that if anything were amiss with a corpse, if only the ruff were not smooth, or the cap did not set right, the corpse in the coffin and beneath the clods would strive to put up its cold hands and arrange it. The bare thought made her nervous.

"Don't talk so, grandmother!" said the girl, shuddering.

"Now," continued the old woman, with singular earnestness, yet smiling strangely at her own folly, "I want one of you, my children — when your mother is dressed and in the coffin — I want one of you to hold a looking glass over my face. Who knows but I may take a glimpse at myself, and see whether all's right?"

"Old and young, we dream of graves and monuments," murmured the stranger youth. "I wonder how mariners feel when the ship is sinking, and they, unknown and undistinguished, are to be buried together in the ocean — that wide and nameless sepulchre?"

For a moment, the old woman's ghastly conception so engrossed the minds of her hearers that a sound abroad in the night, rising like the roar of a blast, had grown broad, deep, and terrible, before the fated group were conscious of it. The house and all within it trembled; the foundations of the earth seemed to be shaken, as if this awful sound were the peal of the last trump. Young and old exchanged one wild glance, and remained an instant, pale, affrighted, without utterance, or power to move. Then the same shriek burst simultaneously from all their lips.

"The Slide! The Slide!"

The simplest words must intimate, but not portray, the unutterable horror of the catastrophe. The victims rushed from their cottage, and sought refuge in what they deemed a safer spot — where, in contemplation of such an emergency, a sort of barrier had been reared. Alas! they had quitted their security, and fled right into the pathway of destruction. Down came the whole side of the mountain, in a cataract of ruin. Just before it reached the house, the stream broke into two branches — shivered not a window there, but overwhelmed the whole vicinity, blocked up the road, and annihilated everything in its dreadful course. Long ere the thunder of the great Slide had ceased to roar among the mountains, the mortal agony had been endured, and the victims were at peace. Their bodies were never found.

The next morning, the light smoke was seen stealing from the cottage chimney up the mountain side. Within, the fire was yet smoldering on the hearth, and the chairs in a circle round it, as if the inhabitants had but gone forth to view the devastation of the Slide, and would shortly return, to thank Heaven for their miraculous escape. All had left separate tokens, by which those who had known the family were made to shed a tear for each. Who has not heard their name? The story has been told far and wide, and will forever be a legend of these mountains. Poets have sung their fate.

There were circumstances which led some to suppose that a stranger had been received into the cottage on this awful night, and had shared the catastrophe of all its inmates. Others denied that there were sufficient grounds for such a conjecture. Woe for the high-souled youth, with his dream of Earthly Immortality! His name and person utterly unknown; his history, his way of life, his plans, a mystery never to be solved, his death and his existence equally a doubt! Whose was the agony of that death moment?

THE WIVES
OF THE DEAD

THE FOLLOWING STORY, the simple and domestic incidents of which may be deemed scarcely worth relating, after such a lapse of time, awakened some degree of interest, a hundred years ago, in a principal seaport of the Bay Province. The rainy twilight of an autumn day — a parlor on the second floor of a small house, plainly furnished, as beseemed the middling circumstances of its inhabitants, yet decorated with little curiosities from beyond the sea, and a few delicate specimens of Indian manufacture — these are the only particulars to be premised in regard to scene and season. Two young and comely women sat together by the fireside, nursing their mutual and peculiar sorrows. They were the recent brides of two brothers, a sailor and a landsman, and two successive days had brought tidings of the death of each, by the chances of Canadian warfare and the tempestuous Atlantic. The universal sympathy excited by this bereavement drew numerous condoling guests to the habitation of the widowed sisters. Several, among whom was the minister, had remained till the verge of evening, when, one by one, whispering many comfortable passages of Scripture that were answered by more abundant tears, they took their leave, and departed to their own happier homes. The mourners, though not insensible to the kindness of their friends, had yearned to be left alone. United, as they had been, by the relationship of the living, and now more closely so by that of the dead, each felt as if whatever consolation her grief admitted were to be found in the bosom of the other. They joined their hearts, and wept together silently. But after an hour of such indulgence, one of the sisters, all of whose emotions were influenced by her mild, quiet, yet not feeble character, began to recollect the precepts of resignation and endurance which piety had taught her, when she did not think to need them. Her misfortune, besides, as earliest known, should earliest cease to interfere with her regular course of duties; accordingly, having placed the table before the fire, and arranged a frugal meal, she took the hand of her companion.

"Come, dearest sister; you have eaten not a morsel today," she said. "Arise, I pray you, and let us ask a blessing on that which is provided for us."

Her sister-in-law was of a lively and irritable

temperament, and the first pangs of her sorrow had been expressed by shrieks and passionate lamentation. She now shrunk from Mary's words, like a wounded sufferer from a hand that revives the throb.

"There is no blessing left for me, neither will I ask it!" cried Margaret, with a fresh burst of tears. "Would it were His will that I might never taste food more!"

Yet she trembled at these rebellious expressions, almost as soon as they were uttered, and, by degrees, Mary succeeded in bringing her sister's mind nearer to the situation of her own. Time went on, and their usual hour of repose arrived. The brothers and their brides, entering the married state with no more than the slender means which then sanctioned such a step, had confederated themselves in one household, with equal rights to the parlor, and claiming exclusive privileges in two sleeping rooms contiguous to it. Thither the widowed ones retired, after heaping ashes upon the dying embers of their fire, and placing a lighted lamp upon the hearth. The doors of both chambers were left open, so that a part of the interior of each, and the beds, with their unclosed curtains, were reciprocally visible. Sleep did not steal upon the sisters at one and the same time. Mary experienced the effect often consequent upon grief quietly borne, and soon sunk into temporary forgetfulness; while Margaret became more disturbed and feverish, in proportion as the night advanced with its deepest and stillest hours. She lay listening to the drops of rain that came down in monotonous succession, unswayed by a breath of wind; and a nervous impulse continually caused her to lift her head from the pillow, and gaze into Mary's chamber and the intermediate apartment. The cold light of the lamp threw the shadows of the furniture up against the wall, stamping them immovably there, except when they were shaken by a sudden flicker of the flame. Two vacant armchairs were in their old positions on opposite sides of the hearth, where the brothers had been wont to sit in young and laughing dignity, as heads of families; two humbler seats were near them, the true thrones of that little empire, where Mary and herself had exercised in love a power that love had won. The cheerful radiance of the fire had shone upon the happy circle, and the dead glimmer of the lamp might have befitted their reunion now. While Margaret groaned in bitterness, she heard a knock at the street-door.

"How would my heart have leapt at that sound but yesterday!" thought she, remembering the anxiety with which she had long awaited tidings from her husband. "I care not for it now; let them begone, for I will not arise."

But even while a sort of childish fretfulness made her thus resolve, she was breathing hurriedly, and straining her ears to catch a repetition of the summons. It is difficult to be convinced of the death of one whom we have deemed another self. The knocking was now renewed in slow and regular strokes, apparently given with the soft end of a doubled fist, and was accompanied by words, faintly heard

through several thicknesses of wall. Margaret
looked to her sister's chamber, and beheld her
still lying in the depths of sleep. She arose,
placed her foot upon the floor, and slightly ar-
rayed herself, trembling between fear and eagerness as she did so.

"Heaven help me!" sighed she. "I have nothing left to fear, and methinks I am ten times
more a coward than ever."

Seizing the lamp from the hearth, she hastened to the window that overlooked the street-
door. It was a lattice, turning upon hinges; and
having thrown it back, she stretched her head a
little way into the moist atmosphere. A lantern
was reddening the front of the house, and melting its light in the neighboring puddles, while a
deluge of darkness overwhelmed every other object. As the window grated on its hinges, a man
in a broadbrimmed hat and blanket-coat stepped
from under the shelter of the projecting story,
and looked upward to discover whom his appli-
cation had aroused. Margaret knew him as a
friendly innkeeper of the town.

"What would you have, Goodman Parker?"
cried the widow.

"Lackaday, is it you, Mistress Margaret?" replied the innkeeper. "I was afraid it might be
your sister Mary; for I hate to see a young
woman in trouble, when I haven't a word of
comfort to whisper her."

"For Heaven's sake, what news do you bring?"
screamed Margaret.

"Why, there has been an express through the
town within this half-hour," said Goodman

Parker, "traveling from the eastern jurisdiction with letters from the governor and council. He tarried at my house to refresh himself with a drop and a morsel, and I asked him what tidings on the frontiers. He tells me we had the better in the skirmish you wot of, and that thirteen men reported slain are well and sound, and your husband among them. Besides, he is appointed of the escort to bring the captivated Frenchers and Indians home to the province jail. I judged you wouldn't mind being broke of your rest, and so I stepped over to tell you. Goodnight."

So saying, the honest man departed; and his lantern gleamed along the street, bringing to view indistinct shapes of things, and the fragments of a world, like order glimmering through chaos, or memory roaming over the past. But Margaret stayed not to watch these picturesque effects. Joy flashed into her heart, and lighted it up at once; and breathless, and with winged steps, she flew to the bedside of her sister. She paused, however, at the door of the chamber, while a thought of pain broke in upon her.

"Poor Mary!" said she to herself. "Shall I waken her, to feel her sorrow sharpened by my happiness? No; I will keep it within my own bosom till the morrow."

She approached the bed, to discover if Mary's sleep were peaceful. Her face was turned partly inward to the pillow, and had been hidden there to weep; but a look of motionless contentment was now visible upon it, as if her heart, like a deep lake, had grown calm because its dead had sunk down so far within. Happy is it, and strange, that the lighter sorrows are those from which dreams are chiefly fabricated. Margaret shrunk from disturbing her sister-in-law, and felt as if her own better fortune had rendered her involuntarily unfaithful, and as if altered and diminished affection must be the consequence of the disclosure she had to make. With a sudden step she turned away. But joy could not long be repressed, even by circumstances that would have excited heavy grief at another moment. Her mind was thronged with delightful thoughts, till sleep stole on, and transformed them to visions, more delightful and more wild, like the breath of winter (but what a cold comparison!) working fantastic tracery upon a window.

When the night was far advanced, Mary awoke with a sudden start. A vivid dream had latterly involved her in its unreal life, of which, however, she could only remember that it had been broken in upon at the most interesting point. For a little time, slumber hung about her like a morning mist, hindering her from perceiving the distinct outline of her situation. She listened with imperfect consciousness to two or three volleys of a rapid and eager knocking; and first she deemed the noise a matter of course, like the breath she drew; next, it appeared a thing in which she had no concern; and lastly, she became aware that it was a summons necessary to be obeyed. At the same moment, the pang of recollection darted into her mind; the pall of sleep was thrown back from the face of grief; the dim light of the chamber, and the objects therein revealed, had retained all her suspended ideas, and restored them as soon as she unclosed her eyes. Again there was a quick peal upon the street-door. Fearing that her sister would also be disturbed, Mary wrapped herself in a cloak and hood, took the lamp from the hearth, and hastened to the window. By some accident, it had been left unhasped, and yielded easily to her hand.

"Who's there?" asked Mary, trembling as she looked forth.

The storm was over, and the moon was up; it shone upon broken clouds above, and below upon houses black with moisture, and upon little lakes of the fallen rain, curling into silver beneath the quick enchantment of a breeze. A young man in a sailor's dress, wet as if he had come out of the depths of the sea, stood alone under the window. Mary recognized him as one whose livelihood was gained by short voyages along the coast; nor did she forget that, previous to her marriage, he had been an unsuccessful wooer of her own.

"What do you seek here, Stephen?" said she.

"Cheer up, Mary, for I seek to comfort you," answered the rejected lover. "You must know I got home not ten minutes ago, and the first thing my good mother told me was the news about your husband. So, without saying a word to the old woman, I clapped on my hat, and ran out of the house. I couldn't have slept a wink before speaking to you, Mary, for the sake of old times."

"Stephen, I thought better of you!" exclaimed

the widow, with gushing tears and preparing to close the lattice; for she was no whit inclined to imitate the first wife of Zadig.*

"But stop, and hear my story out," cried the young sailor. "I tell you we spoke a brig yesterday afternoon, bound in from old England. And whom do you think I saw standing on deck, well and hearty, only a bit thinner than he was five months ago?"

Mary leaned from the window, but could not speak.

"Why, it was your husband himself," continued the generous seaman. "He and three others saved themselves on a spar, when the Blessing turned bottom upward. The brig will beat into the bay by daylight, with this wind, and you'll see him here tomorrow. There's the comfort I bring you, Mary, and so goodnight."

He hurried away, while Mary watched him with a doubt of waking reality, that seemed stronger or weaker as he alternately entered the shade of the houses, or emerged into the broad streaks of moonlight. Gradually, however, a blessed flood of conviction swelled into her heart, in strength to overwhelm her, had its increase been more abrupt. Her first impulse was to rouse her sister-in-law, and communicate the newborn gladness. She opened the chamber door, which had been closed in the course of the night, though not latched, advanced to the bedside, and was about to lay her

* Zadig: a character in Voltaire's novel of the same name. Zadig's wife, believing him dead, is ready to cut off his nose to aid another man.

hand upon the slumberer's shoulder. But then she remembered that Margaret would awake to thoughts of death and woe, rendered not the less bitter by their contrast with her own felicity. She suffered the rays of the lamp to fall upon the unconscious form of the bereaved one. Margaret lay in unquiet sleep, and the drapery was displaced around her; her young cheek was rosy-tinted, and her lips half opened in a vivid smile; an expression of joy, debarred its passage by her sealed eyelids, struggled forth like incense from the whole countenance.

"My poor sister! You will waken too soon from that happy dream," thought Mary.

Before retiring, she set down the lamp, and endeavored to arrange the bedclothes so that the chill air might not do harm to the feverish slumberer. But her hand trembled against Margaret's neck, a tear also fell upon her cheek, and she suddenly awoke.

THE BIRTHMARK

IN THE LATTER PART of the last century there
lived a man of science, an eminent proficient
in every branch of natural philosophy, who not
long before our story opens had made experience
of a spiritual affinity more attractive than any
chemical one. He had left his laboratory to the
care of an assistant, cleared his fine countenance
from the furnace smoke, washed the stain of acids
from his fingers, and persuaded a beautiful
woman to become his wife. In those days when
the comparatively recent discovery of electricity
and other kindred mysteries of Nature seemed
to open paths into the region of miracle, it was
not unusual for the love of science to rival the
love of woman in its depth and absorbing energy.
The higher intellect, the imagination, the spirit,
and even the heart might all find their congenial

aliment in pursuits which, as some of their ardent votaries believed, would ascend from one step of powerful intelligence to another, until the philosopher should lay his hand on the secret of creative force and perhaps make new worlds for himself. We know not whether Aylmer possessed this degree of faith in man's ultimate control over Nature. He had devoted himself, however, too unreservedly to scientific studies ever to be weaned from them by any second passion. His love for his young wife might prove the stronger of the two; but it could only be by intertwining itself with his love of science, and uniting the strength of the latter to his own.

Such a union accordingly took place, and was attended with truly remarkable consequences and a deeply impressive moral. One day, very soon after their marriage, Aylmer sat gazing at his wife with a trouble in his countenance that grew stronger until he spoke.

"Georgiana," said he, "has it never occurred to you that the mark upon your cheek might be removed?"

"No, indeed," said she, smiling; but perceiving the seriousness of his manner, she blushed deeply. "To tell you the truth it has been so often called a charm that I was simple enough to imagine it might be so."

"Ah, upon another face perhaps it might," replied her husband; "but never on yours. No, dearest Georgiana, you came so nearly perfect from the hand of Nature that this slightest possible defect, which we hesitate whether to term a defect or a beauty, shocks me, as being the visible mark of earthly imperfection."

"Shocks you, my husband!" cried Georgiana, deeply hurt; at first reddening with momentary anger, but then bursting into tears. "Then why did you take me from my mother's side? You cannot love what shocks you!"

To explain this conversation it must be mentioned that in the center of Georgiana's left cheek there was a singular mark, deeply interwoven, as it were, with the texture and substance of her face. In the usual state of her complexion — a healthy though delicate bloom — the mark wore a tint of deeper crimson, which imperfectly defined its shape amid the surrounding rosiness. When she blushed it gradually became more indistinct, and finally vanished amid the triumphant rush of blood that bathed the whole cheek with its brilliant glow. But if any shifting motion caused her to turn pale there was the mark again, a crimson stain upon the snow, in what Aylmer sometimes deemed an almost fearful distinctness. Its shape bore not a little similarity to the human hand, though of the smallest pygmy size. Georgiana's lovers were wont to say that some fairy at her birth hour had laid her tiny hand upon the infant's cheek, and left this impress there in token of the magic endowments that were to give her such sway over all hearts. Many a desperate swain would have risked life for the privilege of pressing his lips to the mysterious hand. It must not be concealed, however, that the impression wrought by this fairy sign manual varied exceedingly, ac-

cording to the difference of temperament in the
beholders. Some fastidious persons — but they
were exclusively of her own sex — affirmed that
the bloody hand, as they chose to call it, quite
destroyed the effect of Georgiana's beauty, and
rendered her countenance even hideous. But it
would be as reasonable to say that one of those
small blue stains which sometimes occur in the
purest statuary marble would convert the Eve
of Powers to a monster. Masculine observers, if
the birthmark did not heighten their admiration, contented themselves with wishing it away,
that the world might possess one living speci-
men of ideal loveliness without the semblance of
a flaw. After his marriage — for he thought little
or nothing of the matter before — Aylmer discovered that this was the case with himself.

Had she been less beautiful — if Envy's self
could have found aught else to sneer at — he
might have felt his affection heightened by the
prettiness of this mimic hand, now vaguely por-
trayed, now lost, now stealing forth again and
glimmering to and fro with every pulse of emotion that throbbed within her heart; but seeing
her otherwise so perfect, he found this one defect grow more and more intolerable with every
moment of their united lives. It was the fatal
flaw of humanity which Nature, in one shape
or another, stamps ineffaceably on all her pro-
ductions, either to imply that they are temporary
and finite, or that their perfection must be
wrought by toil and pain. The crimson hand
expressed the ineludible gripe in which mortality clutches the highest and purest of earthly

mold, degrading them into kindred with the lowest, and even with the very brutes, like whom their visible frames return to dust. In this manner, selecting it as the symbol of his wife's liability to sin, sorrow, decay, and death, Aylmer's somber imagination was not long in rendering the birthmark a frightful object, causing him more trouble and horror than ever Georgiana's beauty, whether of soul or sense, had given him delight.

At all the seasons which should have been their happiest, he invariably and without intending it, nay, in spite of a purpose to the contrary, reverted to this one disastrous topic. Trifling as it at first appeared, it so connected itself with innumerable trains of thought and modes of feeling that it became the central point of all. With the morning twilight Aylmer opened his eyes upon his wife's face and recognized the symbol of imperfection; and when they sat together at the evening hearth his eyes wandered stealthily to her cheek, and beheld, flickering with the blaze of the wood fire, the spectral hand that wrote mortality where he would fain have worshiped. Georgiana soon learned to shudder at his gaze. It needed but a glance with the peculiar expression that his face often wore to change the roses of her cheek into a deathlike paleness, amid which the crimson hand was brought strongly out, like a bas-relief of ruby on the whitest marble.

Late one night when the lights were growing dim, so as hardly to betray the stain on the poor wife's cheek, she herself, for the first time, voluntarily took up the subject.

"Do you remember, my dear Aylmer," said she, with a feeble attempt at a smile, "have you any recollection of a dream last night about this odious hand?"

"None! none whatever!" replied Aylmer, starting; but then he added, in a dry, cold tone, affected for the sake of concealing the real depth of his emotion, "I might well dream of it; for before I fell asleep it had taken a pretty firm hold of my fancy."

"And you did dream of it?" continued Georgiana, hastily; for she dreaded lest a gush of tears should interrupt what she had to say. "A terrible dream! I wonder that you can forget it. Is it possible to forget this one expression? 'It is in her heart now; we must have it out!' Reflect, my husband; for by all means I could have you recall that dream."

The mind is in a sad state when Sleep, the all-involving, cannot confine her spectres within the dim region of her sway, but suffers them to break forth, affrighting this actual life with secrets that perchance belong to a deeper one. Aylmer now remembered his dream. He had fancied himself with his servant Aminadab, attempting an operation for the removal of the birthmark; but the deeper went the knife, the deeper sank the hand, until at length its tiny grasp appeared to have caught hold of Georgiana's heart; whence, however, her husband was inexorably resolved to cut or wrench it away.

When the dream had shaped itself perfectly

in his memory, Aylmer sat in his wife's presence
with a guilty feeling. Truth often finds its way to
the mind close muffled in robes of sleep, and
then speaks with uncompromising directness
of matters in regard to which we practice an unconscious self-deception during our waking moments. Until now he had not been aware of the
tyrannizing influence acquired by one idea over
his mind, and of the lengths which he might
find in his heart to go for the sake of giving himself peace.

"Aylmer," resumed Georgiana, solemnly, "I
know not what may be the cost to both of us to
rid me of this fatal birthmark. Perhaps its removal may cause cureless deformity; or it may
be the stain goes as deep as life itself. Again: do
we know that there is a possibility, on any terms,
of unclasping the firm gripe of this little hand
which was laid upon me before I came into the
world?"

"Dearest Georgiana, I have spent much
thought upon the subject," hastily interrupted
Aylmer. "I am convinced of the perfect prac-
ticability of its removal."

"If there be the remotest possibility of it,"
continued Georgiana, "let the attempt be made
at whatever risk. Danger is nothing to me; for
life, while this hateful mark makes me the object
of your horror and disgust, life is a burden
which I would fling down with joy. Either remove this dreadful hand, or take my wretched
life! You have deep science. All the world bears
witness of it. You have achieved great wonders.
Cannot you remove this little, little mark, which

I cover with the tips of two small fingers? Is this beyond your power, for the sake of your own peace, and to save your poor wife from madness?"

"Noblest, dearest, tenderest wife," cried Aylmer, rapturously, "doubt not my power. I have already given this matter the deepest thought — thought which might almost have enlightened me to create a being less perfect than yourself. Georgiana, you have led me deeper than ever into the heart of science. I feel myself fully competent to render this dear cheek as faultless as its fellow; and then, most beloved, what will be my triumph when I shall have corrected what Nature left imperfect in her fairest work! Even Pygmalion, when his sculptured woman assumed life, felt not greater ecstasy than mine will be."

"It is resolved, then," said Georgiana, faintly smiling. "And, Aylmer, spare me not, though you should find the birthmark take refuge in my heart at last."

Her husband tenderly kissed her cheek — her right cheek — not that which bore the impress of the crimson hand.

The next day Aylmer apprised his wife of a plan that he had formed whereby he might have opportunity for the intense thought and constant watchfulness which the proposed operation would require; while Georgiana, likewise, would enjoy the perfect repose essential to its success. They were to seclude themselves in the extensive apartments occupied by Aylmer as a laboratory, and where, during his toilsome youth, he had made discoveries in the elemental powers of Nature that had roused the admiration of all the learned societies in Europe. Seated calmly in this laboratory, the pale philosopher had investigated the secrets of the highest cloud region and of the profoundest mines; he had satisfied himself of the causes that kindled and kept alive the fires of the volcano; and had explained the mystery of fountains, and how it is that they gush forth, some so bright and pure, and others with such rich medicinal virtues, from the dark bosom of the earth. Here, too, at an earlier period, he had studied the wonders of the human frame, and attempted to fathom the very process by which Nature assimilates all her precious influences from earth and air, and from the spiritual world, to create and foster man, her masterpiece. The latter pursuit, however, Aylmer had long laid aside in unwilling recognition of the truth — against which all seekers sooner or later stumble — that our great creative Mother, while she amuses us with apparently working in the broadest sunshine, is yet severely careful to keep her own secrets, and, in spite of her pretended openness, shows us nothing but results. She permits us, indeed, to mar, but seldom to mend, and, like a jealous patentee, on no account to make. Now, however, Aylmer resumed these half-forgotten investigations; not, of course, with such hopes or wishes as first suggested them; but because they involved much physiological truth and lay in the path of his proposed scheme for the treatment of Georgiana.

As he led her over the threshold of the laboratory, Georgiana was cold and tremulous. Aylmer looked cheerfully into her face, with intent to reassure her, but was so startled with the intense glow of the birthmark upon the whiteness of her cheek that he could not restrain a strong convulsive shudder. His wife fainted.

"Aminadab! Aminadab!" shouted Aylmer, stamping violently on the floor.

Forthwith there issued from an inner apartment a man of low stature, but bulky frame, with shaggy hair hanging about his visage, which was grimed with the vapors of the furnace. This personage had been Aylmer's underworker during his whole scientific career, and was admirably fitted for that office by his great mechanical readiness, and the skill with which, while incapable of comprehending a single principle, he executed all the details of his master's experiments. With his vast strength, his shaggy hair, his smoky aspect, and the indescribable earthiness that encrusted him, he seemed to represent man's physical nature; while Aylmer's slender figure and pale, intellectual face were no less apt a type of the spiritual element.

"Throw open the door of the boudoir, Aminadab," said Aylmer, "and burn a pastil."

"Yes, master," answered Aminadab, looking intently at the lifeless form of Georgiana; and then he muttered to himself, "If she were my wife, I'd never part with that birthmark."

When Georgiana recovered consciousness she found herself breathing an atmosphere of penetrating fragrance, the gentle potency of which had recalled her from her deathlike faintness.

The scene around her looked like enchantment. Aylmer had converted those smoky, dingy, somber rooms, where he had spent his brightest years in recondite pursuits, into a series of beautiful apartments not unfit to be the secluded abode of a lovely woman. The walls were hung with gorgeous curtains, which imparted the combination of grandeur and grace that no other species of adornment can achieve; and as they fell from the ceiling to the floor, their rich and ponderous folds, concealing all angles and straight lines, appeared to shut in the scene from infinite space. For aught Georgiana knew, it might be a pavilion among the clouds. And Aylmer, excluding the sunshine, which would have interfered with his chemical processes, had supplied its place with perfumed lamps, emitting flames of various hue, but all uniting in a soft, impurpled radiance. He now knelt by his wife's side, watching her earnestly, but without alarm; for he was confident in his science, and felt that he could draw a magic circle round her within which no evil might intrude.

"Where am I? Ah, I remember," said Georgiana, faintly; and she placed her hand over her cheek to hide the terrible mark from her husband's eyes.

"Fear not, dearest!" exclaimed he. "Do not shrink from me! Believe me, Georgiana, I even rejoice in this single imperfection, since it will be such a rapture to remove it."

"Oh, spare me!" sadly replied his wife. "Pray do not look at it again. I never can forget that convulsive shudder."

In order to soothe Georgiana, and, as it were, to release her mind from the burden of actual things, Aylmer now put in practice some of the light and playful secrets which science had taught him among its profounder lore. Airy figures, absolutely bodiless ideas, and forms of unsubstantial beauty came and danced before her, imprinting their momentary footsteps on beams of light. Though she had some indistinct idea of the method of these optical phenomena, still the illusion was almost perfect enough to warrant the belief that her husband possessed sway over the spiritual world. Then again, when she felt a wish to look forth from her seclusion, immediately, as if her thoughts were answered, the procession of external existence flitted across a screen. The scenery and the figures of actual life were perfectly represented, but with that bewitching, yet indescribable difference which always makes a picture, an image, or a shadow so much more attractive than the original. When wearied of this, Aylmer bade her cast her eyes upon a vessel containing a quantity of earth. She did so, with little interest at first; but was soon startled to perceive the germ of a plant shooting upward from the soil. Then came the slender stalk; the leaves gradually unfolded themselves; and amid them was a perfect and lovely flower.

"It is magical!" cried Georgiana. "I dare not touch it."

"Nay, pluck it," answered Aylmer, "pluck it, and inhale its brief perfume while you may. The flower will wither in a few moments and leave nothing save its brown seed vessels; but thence may be perpetuated a race as ephemeral as it-self."

But Georgiana had no sooner touched the flower than the whole plant suffered a blight, its leaves turning coal black as if by the agency of fire.

"There was too powerful a stimulus," said Aylmer, thoughtfully.

To make up for this abortive experiment, he proposed to take her portrait by a scientific process of his own invention. It was to be effected by rays of light striking upon a polished plate of metal. Georgiana assented; but, on looking at the result, was affrighted to find the features of the portrait blurred and indefinable; while the minute figure of a hand appeared where the cheek should have been. Aylmer snatched the metallic plate and threw it into a jar of corrosive acid.

Soon, however, he forgot these mortifying failures. In the intervals of study and chemical experiment he came to her flushed and exhausted, but seemed invigorated by her presence, and spoke in glowing language of the resources of his art. He gave a history of the long dynasty of the alchemists, who spent so many ages in quest of the universal solvent by which the golden principle might be elicited from all things vile and base. Aylmer appeared to believe that, by the plainest scientific logic, it was altogether within the limits of possibility to discover this long-sought medium; "but," he added, "a philosopher who should go deep enough to acquire the power would attain too lofty a wisdom to stoop to the exercise of it. " Not less singular were his opinions in regard to the elixir vitæ. He more than intimated that it was at his option to concoct a liquid that should prolong life for years, perhaps interminably; but that it would produce a discord in Nature which all the world, and chiefly the quaffer of the immortal nostrum, would find cause to curse.

"Aylmer, are you in earnest?" asked Georgiana, looking at him with amazement and fear. "It is terrible to possess such power, or even to dream of possessing it."

"Oh, do not tremble, my love," said her husband. "I would not wrong either you or myself by working such inharmonious effects upon our lives; but I would have you consider how trifling, in comparison, is the skill requisite to remove this little hand."

At the mention of the birthmark, Georgiana, as usual, shrank as if a redhot iron had touched her cheek.

Again Aylmer applied himself to his labors. She could hear his voice in the distant furnace room giving directions to Aminadab, whose harsh, uncouth, misshapen tones were audible in response, more like the grunt or growl of a brute than human speech. After hours of absence, Aylmer reappeared and proposed that she should now examine his cabinet of chemical products and natural treasures of the earth. Among the former he showed her a small vial, in which, he remarked, was contained a gentle yet most powerful fragrance, capable of impregnating all the breezes that blow across a kingdom. They were of inestimable value, the contents of that little vial; and, as he said so, he threw some of the perfume into the air and filled the room with piercing and invigorating delight.

"And what is this?" asked Georgiana, pointing to a small crystal globe containing a gold-colored liquid. "It is so beautiful to the eye that I could imagine it the elixir of life."

"In one sense it is," replied Aylmer; "or rather, the elixir of immortality. It is the most precious poison that ever was concocted in this world. By its aid I could apportion the lifetime of any mortal at whom you might point your finger. The strength of the dose would determine whether he were to linger out years, or drop dead in the midst of a breath. No king on his guarded throne could keep his life if I, in my private station, should deem that the welfare of millions justified me in depriving him of it."

"Why do you keep such a terrific drug?" inquired Georgiana in horror.

"Do not mistrust me, dearest," said her husband, smiling; "its virtuous potency is yet greater than its harmful one. But see! here is a powerful cosmetic. With a few drops of this in a vase of water, freckles may be washed away as easily as the hands are cleansed. A stronger infusion would take the blood out of the cheek, and leave the rosiest beauty a pale ghost."

"Is it with this lotion that you intend to bathe my cheek?" asked Georgiana, anxiously.

"Oh, no," hastily replied her husband; "this

is merely superficial. Your case demands a remedy that shall go deeper."

In his interviews with Georgiana, Aylmer generally made minute inquiries as to her sensations and whether the confinement of the rooms and the temperature of the atmosphere agreed with her. These questions had such a particular drift that Georgiana began to conjecture that she was already subjected to certain physical influences, either breathed in with the fragrant air or taken with her food. She fancied likewise, but it might be altogether fancy, that there was a stirring up of her system — a strange, indefinite sensation creeping through her veins, and tingling, half painfully, half pleasurably, at her heart. Still, whenever she dared to look into the mirror, there she beheld herself pale as a white rose and with the crimson birthmark stamped upon her cheek. Not even Aylmer now hated it so much as she.

To dispel the tedium of the hours which her husband found it necessary to devote to the processes of combination and analysis, Georgiana turned over the volumes of his scientific library. In many dark old tomes she met with chapters full of romance and poetry. They were the works of philosophers of the middle ages, such as Albertus Magnus, Cornelius Agrippa, Paracelsus, and the famous friar who created the prophetic Brazen Head. All these antique naturalists stood in advance of their centuries, yet were imbued with some of their credulity, and therefore were believed, and perhaps imagined themselves to have acquired from the investigation of Nature

.a power above Nature, and from physics a sway over the spiritual world. Hardly less curious and imaginative were the early volumes of the Transactions of the Royal Society, in which the members, knowing little of the limits of natural possibility, were continually recording wonders or proposing methods whereby wonders might be wrought.

But to Georgiana the most engrossing volume was a large folio from her husband's own hand, in which he had recorded every experiment of his scientific career, its original aim, the methods adopted for its development, and its final success or failure, with the circumstances to which either event was attributable. The book, in truth, was both the history and emblem of his ardent, ambitious, imaginative, yet practical and laborious life. He handled physical details as if there were nothing beyond them; yet spiritualized them all, and redeemed himself from materialism by his strong and eager aspiration toward the infinite. In his grasp the veriest clod of earth assumed a soul. Georgiana, as she read, reverenced Aylmer and loved him more profoundly than ever, but with a less entire dependence on his judgment than heretofore. Much as he had accomplished, she could not but observe that his most splendid successes were almost invariably failures, if compared with the ideal at which he aimed. His brightest diamonds were the merest pebbles, and felt to be so by himself, in comparison with the inestimable gems which lay hidden beyond his reach. The volume, rich with achievements that had won renown for its author, was yet as melancholy a record as ever mortal hand had penned. It was the sad confession and continual exemplification of the shortcomings of the composite man, the spirit burdened with clay and working in matter, and of the despair that assails the higher nature at finding itself so miserably thwarted by the earthly part. Perhaps every man of genius in whatever sphere might recognize the image of his own experience in Aylmer's journal.

So deeply did these reflections affect Georgiana that she laid her face upon the open volume and burst into tears. In this situation she was found by her husband.

"It is dangerous to read in a sorcerer's books," said he with a smile, though his countenance was uneasy and displeased. "Georgiana, there are pages in that volume which I can scarcely glance over and keep my senses. Take heed lest it prove as detrimental to you."

"It has made me worship you more than ever," said she.

"Ah, wait for this one success," rejoined he, "then worship me if you will. I shall deem myself hardly unworthy of it. But come, I have sought you for the luxury of your voice. Sing to me, dearest."

So she poured out the liquid music of her voice to quench the thirst of his spirit. He then took his leave with a boyish exuberance of gaiety, assuring her that her seclusion would endure but a little longer, and that the result was already certain. Scarcely had he departed when Georgiana felt irresistibly impelled to follow him.

She had forgotten to inform Aylmer of a symptom which for two or three hours past had begun to excite her attention. It was a sensation in the fatal birthmark, not painful, but which induced a restlessness throughout her system. Hastening after her husband, she intruded for the first time into the laboratory.

The first thing that struck her eye was the furnace, that hot and feverish worker, with the intense glow of its fire, which by the quantities of soot clustered above it seemed to have been burning for ages. There was a distilling apparatus in full operation. Around the room were retorts, tubes, cylinders, crucibles, and other apparatus of chemical research. An electrical machine stood ready for immediate use. The atmosphere felt oppressively close, and was tainted with gaseous odors which had been tormented forth by the processes of science. The severe and homely simplicity of the apartment, with its naked walls and brick pavement, looked strange, accustomed as Georgiana had become to the fantastic elegance of her boudoir. But what chiefly, indeed almost solely, drew her attention, was the aspect of Aylmer himself.

He was pale as death, anxious and absorbed, and hung over the furnace as if it depended upon his utmost watchfulness whether the liquid which it was distilling should be the draught of immortal happiness or misery. How different from the sanguine and joyous mien that he had assumed for Georgiana's encouragement!

"Carefully now, Aminadab; carefully, thou human machine; carefully, thou man of clay!"

muttered Aylmer, more to himself than his assistant. "Now, if there be a thought too much or too little, it is all over."

"Ho! ho!" mumbled Aminadab. "Look, master! look!"

Aylmer raised his eyes hastily, and at first reddened, then grew paler than ever, on beholding Georgiana. He rushed toward her and seized her arm with a grip that left the print of his fingers upon it.

"Why do you come hither? Have you no trust in your husband?" cried he, impetuously. "Would you throw the blight of that fatal birthmark over my labors? It is not well done. Go, prying woman, go!"

"Nay, Aylmer," said Georgiana with the firmness of which she possessed no stinted endowment, "it is not you that have a right to complain. You mistrust your wife; you have concealed the anxiety with which you watch the development of this experiment. Think not so unworthily of me, my husband. Tell me all the risk we run, and fear not that I shall shrink; for my share in it is far less than your own."

"No, no, Georgiana!" said Aylmer, impatiently; "it must not be."

"I submit," replied she calmly. "And, Aylmer, I shall quaff whatever draught you bring me; but it will be on the same principle that would induce me to take a dose of poison if offered by your hand."

"My noble wife," said Aylmer, deeply moved, "I knew not the height and depth of your nature until now. Nothing shall be concealed.

Know, then, that this crimson hand, superficial as it seems, has clutched its grasp into your being with a strength of which I had no previous conception. I have already administered agents powerful enough to do aught except to change your entire physical system. Only one thing remains to be tried. If that fail us we are ruined."

"Why did you hesitate to tell me this?" asked she.

"Because, Georgiana," said Aylmer, in a low voice, "there is danger."

"Danger? There is but one danger — that this horrible stigma shall be left upon my cheek!" cried Georgiana. "Remove it, remove it, whatever be the cost, or we shall both go mad!"

"Heaven knows your words are too true," said Aylmer, sadly. "And now, dearest, return to your boudoir. In a little while all will be tested."

He conducted her back and took leave of her with a solemn tenderness which spoke far more than his words how much was now at stake. After his departure Georgiana became rapt in musings. She considered the character of Aylmer, and did it completer justice than at any previous moment. Her heart exulted, while it trembled, at his honorable love — so pure and lofty that it would accept nothing less than perfection nor miserably make itself contented with an earthlier nature than he had dreamed of. She felt how much more precious was such a sentiment than that meaner kind which would have borne with the imperfection for her sake, and have been guilty of treason to holy love by degrading its perfect idea to the level of the actual; and with her whole spirit she prayed that, for a single moment, she might satisfy his highest and deepest conception. Longer than one moment she well knew it could not be; for his spirit was ever on the march, ever ascending, and each instant required something that was beyond the scope of the instant before.

The sound of her husband's footsteps aroused her. He bore a crystal goblet containing a liquor colorless as water, but bright enough to be the draught of immortality. Aylmer was pale; but it seemed rather the consequence of a highly wrought state of mind and tension of spirit than of fear or doubt.

"The concoction of the draught has been perfect," said he, in answer to Georgiana's look. "Unless all my science have deceived me, it cannot fail."

"Save on your account, my dearest Aylmer," observed his wife, "I might wish to put off this birthmark of mortality by relinquishing mortality itself in preference to any other mode. Life is but a sad possession to those who have attained precisely the degree of moral advancement at which I stand. Were I weaker and blinder it might be happiness. Were I stronger, it might be endured hopefully. But, being what I find myself, methinks I am of all mortals the most fit to die."

"You are fit for heaven without tasting death!" replied her husband. "But why do we speak of dying? The draught cannot fail. Behold its effect upon this plant."

On the window seat there stood a geranium

diseased with yellow blotches, which had over-spread all its leaves. Aylmer poured a small quantity of the liquid upon the soil in which it grew. In a little time, when the roots of the plant had taken up the moisture, the unsightly blotches began to be extinguished in a living verdure.

"There needed no proof," said Georgiana, quietly. "Give me the goblet. I joyfully stake all upon your word."

"Drink, then, thou lofty creature!" exclaimed Aylmer, with fervid admiration. "There is no taint of imperfection on thy spirit. Thy sensible frame, too, shall soon be all perfect."

She quaffed the liquid and returned the goblet to his hand.

"It is grateful," said she with a placid smile. "Methinks it is like water from a heavenly fountain; for it contains I know not what of unobtrusive fragrance and deliciousness. It allays a feverish thirst that had parched me for many days. Now, dearest, let me sleep. My earthly senses are closing over my spirit like the leaves around the heart of a rose at sunset."

She spoke the last words with a gentle reluctance, as if it required almost more energy than she could command to pronounce the faint and lingering syllables. Scarcely had they loitered through her lips ere she was lost in slumber. Aylmer sat by her side, watching her aspect with the emotions proper to a man the whole value of whose existence was involved in the process now to be tested. Mingled with this mood, however, was the philosophic investigation characteristic of the man of science. Not the minutest symptom escaped him. A heightened flush of the cheek, a slight irregularity of breath, a quiver of the eyelid, a hardly perceptible tremor through the frame — such were the details which, as the moments passed, he wrote down in his folio volume. Intense thought had set its stamp upon every previous page of that volume, but the thoughts of years were all concentrated upon the last.

While thus employed, he failed not to gaze often at the fatal hand, and not without a shudder. Yet once, by a strange and unaccountable impulse, he pressed it with his lips. His spirit recoiled, however, in the very act; and Georgiana, out of the midst of her deep sleep, moved uneasily and murmured as if in remonstrance. Again Aylmer resumed his watch. Nor was it without avail. The crimson hand, which at first had been strongly visible upon the marble paleness of Georgiana's cheek, now grew more faintly outlined. She remained not less pale than ever; but the birthmark, with every breath that came and went, lost somewhat of its former distinctness. Its presence had been awful; its departure was more awful still. Watch the stain of the rainbow fading out the sky, and you will know how that mysterious symbol passed away.

"By Heaven! it is well-nigh gone!" said Aylmer to himself, in almost irrepressible ecstasy. "I can scarcely trace it now. Success! success! And now it is like the faintest rose color. The lightest flush of blood across her cheek would overcome it. But she is so pale!"

He drew aside the window curtain and suffered the light of natural day to fall into the room and rest upon her cheek. At the same time he heard a gross, hoarse chuckle, which he had long known as his servant Aminadab's expression of delight.

"Ah, clod! ah, earthly mass!" cried Aylmer, laughing in a sort of frenzy, "you have served me well! Matter and spirit — earth and heaven — have both done their part in this! Laugh, thing of the senses! You have earned the right to laugh."

These exclamations broke Georgiana's sleep. She slowly unclosed her eyes and gazed into the mirror which her husband had arranged for that purpose. A faint smile flitted over her lips when she recognized how barely perceptible was now that crimson hand which had once blazed forth with such disastrous brilliancy as to scare away all their happiness. But then her eyes sought Aylmer's face with a trouble and anxiety that he could by no means account for.

"My poor Aylmer!" murmured she.

"Poor? Nay, richest, happiest, most favored!" exclaimed he. "My peerless bride, it is successful! You are perfect!"

"My poor Aylmer," she repeated, with a more than human tenderness, "you have aimed loftily; you have done nobly. Do not repent that with so high and pure a feeling, you have rejected the best the earth could offer. Aylmer, dearest Aylmer, I am dying!"

Alas! It was too true! The fatal hand had grappled with the mystery of life, and was the bond by which an angelic spirit kept itself in union with a mortal frame. As the last crimson tint of the birthmark — that sole token of human imperfection — faded from her cheek, the parting breath of the now perfect woman passed into the atmosphere, and her soul, lingering a moment near her husband, took its heavenward flight. Then a hoarse, chuckling laugh was heard again! Thus ever does the gross fatality of earth exult in its invariable triumph over the immortal essence which, in this dim sphere of half development, demands the completeness of a higher state. Yet, had Aylmer reached a profounder wisdom, he need not thus have flung away the happiness which would have woven his mortal life of the selfsame texture with the celestial. The momentary circumstance was too strong for him; he failed to look beyond the shadowy scope of time, and, living once for all in eternity, to find the perfect future in the present.

ROGER MALVIN'S BURIAL

ONE OF THE FEW INCIDENTS of Indian warfare naturally susceptible of the moonlight of romance was that expedition undertaken for the defence of the frontiers in the year 1725, which resulted in the well-remembered "Lovell's Fight." Imagination, by casting certain circumstances judicially into the shade, may see much to admire in the heroism of a little band who gave battle to twice their number in the heart of the enemy's country. The open bravery displayed by both parties was in accordance with civilized ideas of valor; and chivalry itself might not blush to record the deeds of one or two individuals. The battle, though so fatal to those who fought, was not unfortunate in its consequences to the country; for it broke the strength of a tribe and conduced to the peace which subsisted during several ensuing years. History and tradition are unusually minute in their memorials of their affair; and the captain of a scouting party of frontier men has acquired as actual a military renown as many a victorious leader of thousands. Some of the incidents contained in the following pages will be recognized, notwithstanding the substitution of fictitious names, by such as have heard, from old men's lips, the fate of the few combatants who were in a condition to retreat after "Lovell's Fight."

The early sunbeams hovered cheerfully upon the treetops, beneath which two weary and wounded men had stretched their limbs the night before. Their bed of withered oak leaves was strewn upon the small level space, at the foot of a rock, situated near the summit of one of the gentle swells by which the face of the country is there diversified. The mass of granite, rearing its smooth, flat surface fifteen or twenty feet above their heads, was not unlike a gigantic gravestone, upon which the veins seemed to form an inscription in forgotten characters. On a tract of several acres around this rock, oaks and other hard-wood trees had supplied the place of the pines, which were the usual growth of the land; and a young and vigorous sapling stood close beside the travelers.

The severe wound of the elder man had probably deprived him of sleep; for, so soon as the first ray of sunshine rested on the top of the highest tree, he reared himself painfully from his recumbent posture and sat erect. The deep

lines of his countenance and the scattered gray
of his hair marked him as past the middle age;
but his muscular frame would, but for the effect
of his wound, have been as capable of sustaining fatigue as in the early vigor of life. Languor
and exhaustion now sat upon his haggard
features; and the despairing glance which he
sent forward through the depths of the forest
proved his own conviction that his pilgrimage
was at an end. He next turned his eyes to the
companion who reclined by his side. The
youth — for he had scarcely attained the years
of manhood — lay, with his head upon his arm,
in the embrace of an unquiet sleep, which a
thrill of pain from his wounds seemed each moment on the point of breaking. His right hand
grasped a musket; and, to judge from the violent
action of his features, his slumbers were bringing
back a vision of the conflict of which he was one
of the few survivors. A shout — deep and loud
in his dreaming fancy — found its way in an imperfect murmur to his lips; and, starting even
at the slight sound of his own voice, he suddenly
awoke. The first act of reviving recollection was
to make anxious inquiries respecting the condition of his wounded fellow traveler. The latter
shook his head.

"Reuben, my boy," said he, "this rock beneath
which we sit will serve for an old hunter's gravestone. There is many and many a long mile of
howling wilderness before us yet; nor would
it avail me anything if the smoke of my own
chimney were but on the other side of that swell

of land. The Indian bullet was deadlier than I thought."

"You are weary with our three days' travel," replied the youth, "and a little longer rest will recruit you. Sit you here while I search the woods for the herbs and roots that must be our sustenance; and, having eaten, you shall lean on me, and we will turn our faces homeward. I doubt not that, with my help, you can attain to some one of the frontier garrisons."

"There is not two days' life in me, Reuben," said the other, calmly, "and I will no longer burden you with my useless body, when you can scarcely support your own. Your wounds are deep and your strength is failing fast; yet, if you hasten onward alone, you may be preserved. For me there is no hope, and I will await death here."

"If it must be so, I will remain and watch by you," said Reuben, resolutely.

"No, my son, no," rejoined his companion. "Let the wish of a dying man have weight with you; give me one grasp of your hand, and get you hence. Think you that my last moments will be eased by the thought that I leave you to die a more lingering death? I have loved you like a father, Reuben; and at a time like this I should have something of a father's authority. I charge you to be gone that I may die in peace."

"And because you have been a father to me, should I therefore leave you to perish and to lie unburied in the wilderness?" exclaimed the youth. "No; if your end be in truth approaching, I will watch by you and receive your parting words. I will dig a grave here by the rock, in

which, if my weakness overcome me, we will
rest together; or, if Heaven gives me strength, I
will seek my way home."

"In the cities and wherever men dwell," replied the other, "they bury their dead in the
earth; they hide them from the sight of the living; but here, where no step may pass perhaps
for a hundred years, wherefore should I not
rest beneath the open sky, covered only by the
oak leaves when the autumn winds shall strew
them? And for a monument, here is this gray
rock, on which my dying hand shall carve the
name of Roger Malvin; and the traveler in days
to come will know that here sleeps a hunter and
a warrior. Tarry not, then, for a folly like
this, but hasten away, if not for your own sake,
for hers who will else be desolate."

Malvin spoke the last few words in a faltering voice, and their effect upon his companion
was strongly visible. They reminded him that
there were other and less questionable duties
than that of sharing the fate of a man whom his
death could not benefit. Nor can it be affirmed
that no selfish feeling strove to enter Reuben's
heart, though the consciousness made him more
earnestly resist his companion's entreaties.

"How terrible to wait the slow approach of
death in this solitude!" exclaimed he. "A brave
man does not shrink in the battle; and, when
friends stand round the bed, even women may
die composedly; but here — "

"I shall not shrink even here, Reuben
Bourne," interrupted Malvin. "I am a man of
no weak heart, and, if I were, there is a surer

support than that of earthly friends. You are young, and life is dear to you. Your last moments will need comfort far more than mine; and when you have laid me in the earth, and are alone, and night is settling on the forest, you will feel all the bitterness of the death that may now be escaped. But I will urge no selfish motive to your generous nature. Leave me for my sake, that, having said a prayer for your safety, I may have space to settle my account undisturbed by worldly sorrows."

"And your daughter — how shall I dare to meet her eye?" exclaimed Reuben. "She will ask the fate of her father, whose life I vowed to defend with my own. Must I tell her that he traveled three days' march with me from the field of battle and that then I left him to perish in the wilderness? Were it not better to lie down and die by your side than to return safe and say this to Dorcas?"

"Tell my daughter," said Roger Malvin, "that, though yourself sore wounded, and weak, and weary, you led my tottering footsteps many a mile, and left me only at my earnest entreaty, because I would not have your blood upon my soul. Tell her that through pain and danger you were faithful, and that, if your life-blood could have saved me, it would have flowed to its last drop; and tell her that you will be something dearer than a father, and that my blessing is with you both, and that my dying eyes can see a long and pleasant path in which you will journey together."

As Malvin spoke he almost raised himself

from the ground, and the energy of his con-
cluding words seemed to fill the wild and lonely
forest with a vision of happiness; but, when he
sank exhausted upon his bed of oak leaves, the
light which had kindled in Reuben's eyes was
quenched. He felt as if it were both sin and
folly to think of happiness at such a moment.
His companion watched his changing countenance, and sought with generous art to wile him
to his own good.

"Perhaps I deceive myself in regard to the
time I have to live," he resumed. "It may be
that, with speedy assistance, I might recover of
my wound. The foremost fugitives must, ere this,
have carried tidings of our fatal battle to the
frontiers, and parties will be out to succor those
in like condition with ourselves. Should you
meet one of these and guide them hither, who
can tell but that I may sit by my own fireside
again?"

A mournful smile strayed across the features
of the dying man as he insinuated that un-
founded hope, which, however, was not without
its effect on Reuben. No merely selfish motive,
nor even the desolate condition of Dorcas, could
have induced him to desert his companion at
such a moment — but his wishes seized on
the thought that Malvin's life might be preserved, and his sanguine nature heightened almost to certainty the remote possibility of pro-
curing human aid.

"Surely there is reason, weighty reason, to
hope that friends are not far distant," he said,
half aloud. "There fled one coward, un-

wounded, in the beginning of the fight, and most probably he made good speed. Every true man on the frontier would shoulder his musket at the news; and, though no party may range so far into the woods as this, I shall perhaps encounter them in one day's march. Counsel me faithfully," he added, turning to Malvin, in distrust of his own motives. "Were your situation mine, would you desert me while life remained?"

"It is now twenty years," replied Roger Malvin, — sighing, however, as he secretly acknowledged the wide dissimilarity between the two cases, — "it is now twenty years since I escaped with one dear friend from Indian captivity near Montreal. We journeyed many days through the woods, till at length overcome with hunger and weariness, my friend lay down and besought me to leave him; for he knew that, if I remained, we both must perish; and, with but little hope of obtaining succor, I heaped a pillow of dry leaves beneath his head and hastened on."

"And did you return in time to save him?" asked Reuben, hanging on Malvin's words as if they were to be prophetic of his own success.

"I did," answered the other. "I came upon the camp of a hunting party before sunset of the same day. I guided them to the spot where my comrade was expecting death; and he is now a hale and hearty man upon his own farm, far within the frontiers, while I lie wounded here in the depths of the wilderness."

This example, powerful in affecting Reuben's decision, was aided, unconsciously to himself, by the hidden strength of many another motive. Roger Malvin perceived that the victory was nearly won.

"Now, go, my son, and Heaven prosper you!" he said. "Turn not back with your friends when you meet them, lest your wounds and weariness overcome you; but send hitherward two or three, that may be spared, to search for me; and believe me, Reuben, my heart will be lighter with every step you take toward home." Yet there was, perhaps, a change both in his countenance and voice as he spoke thus; for, after all, it was a ghastly fate to be left expiring in the wilderness.

Reuben Bourne, but half convinced that he was acting rightly, at length raised himself from the ground and prepared himself for his departure. And first, though contrary to Malvin's wishes, he collected a stock of roots and herbs, which had been their only food during the last two days. This useless supply he placed within reach of the dying man, for whom, also, he swept together a bed of dry oak leaves. Then climbing to the summit of the rock, which on one side was rough and broken, he bent the oak sapling downward, and bound his handkerchief to the topmost branch. This precaution was not unnecessary to direct any who might come in search of Malvin; for every part of the rock, except its broad, smooth front, was concealed at a little distance by the dense undergrowth of the forest. The handkerchief had been the bandage of a wound upon Reuben's arm; and, as he bound it to the tree, he vowed by the blood that

stained it that he would return, either to save his
companion's life or to lay his body in the grave.
He then descended, and stood, with downcast
eyes, to receive Roger Malvin's parting words.

The experience of the latter suggested much
and minute advice respecting the youth's journey through the trackless forest. Upon this subject he spoke with calm earnestness, as if he were
sending Reuben to the battle or the chase
while he himself remained secure at home, and
not as if the human countenance that was about
to leave him were the last he would ever behold.
But his firmness was shaken before he concluded.

"Carry my blessing to Dorcas, and say that my
last prayer shall be for her and you. Bid her to
have no hard thoughts because you left me
here," — Reuben's heart smote him — "for that
your life would not have weighed with you if its
sacrifice could have done me good. She will
marry you after she has mourned a little while
for her father; and Heaven grant you long and
happy days, and may your children's children
stand round your death bed! And, Reuben,"
added he, as the weakness of mortality made its
way at last, "return, when your wounds are
healed and your weariness refreshed — return
to this wild rock, and lay my bones in the grave,
and say a prayer over them."

An almost superstitious regard, arising perhaps from the customs of the Indians, whose
war was with the dead as well as the living, was
paid by the frontier inhabitants to the rites of
sepulture; and there are many instances of the
sacrifice of life in the attempt to bury those who

had fallen by the "sword of the wilderness." Reuben, therefore, felt the full importance of the promise which he most solemnly made to return and perform Roger Malvin's obsequies. It was remarkable that the latter, speaking his whole heart in his parting words, no longer endeavored to persuade the youth that even the speediest succor might avail to the preservation of his life. Reuben was internally convinced that he should see Malvin's living face no more. His generous nature would fain have delayed him, at whatever risk, till the dying scene were past; but the desire of existence and the hope of happiness had strengthened in his heart, and he was unable to resist them.

"It is enough," said Roger Malvin, having listened to Reuben's promise. "Go, and God speed you!"

The youth pressed his hand in silence, turned, and was departing. His slow and faltering steps, however, had borne him but a little way before Malvin's voice recalled him.

"Reuben, Reuben," said he, faintly; and Reuben returned and knelt down by the dying man.

"Raise me, and let me lean against the rock," was his last request. "My face will be turned toward home, and I shall see you a moment longer as you pass among the trees."

Reuben, having made the desired alteration in his companion's posture, again began his solitary pilgrimage. He walked more hastily at first than was consistent with his strength; for a sort of guilty feeling, which sometimes torments men in their most justifiable acts, caused him to

seek concealment from Malvin's eyes; but after
he had trodden far upon the rustling forest
leaves he crept back, impelled by a wild and
painful curiosity, and, sheltered by the earthy
roots of an uptorn tree, gazed earnestly at the
desolate man. The morning sun was unclouded,
and the trees and shrubs imbibed the sweet air
of the month of May; yet there seemed a gloom
on Nature's face, as if she sympathized with mortal pain and sorrow. Roger Malvin's hands were
uplifted in a fervent prayer, some of the words
of which stole through the stillness of the woods
and entered Reuben's heart, torturing it with
an unutterable pang. They were the broken accents of a petition for his own happiness and
that of Dorcas; and, as the youth listened, conscience, or something in its similitude, pleaded
strongly with him to return and lie down again
by the rock. He felt how hard was the doom of
the kind and generous being whom he had deserted in his extremity. Death would come like
the slow approach of a corpse, stealing gradually
toward him through the forest, and showing
its ghastly and motionless features from behind
a nearer and yet a nearer tree. But such must
have been Reuben's own fate had he tarried another sunset; and who shall impute blame to
him if he shrink from so useless a sacrifice? As
he gave a parting look, a breeze waved the little banner upon the sapling oak and reminded
Reuben of his vow.

Many circumstances combined to retard the
wounded traveler in his way to the frontiers. On

the second day the clouds, gathering densely over the sky, precluded the possibility of regulating his course by the position of the sun; and he knew not but that every effort of his almost exhausted strength was removing him farther from the home he sought. His scanty sustenance was supplied by the berries and other spontaneous products of the forest. Herds of deer, it is true, sometimes bounded past him, and partridges frequently whirred up before his footsteps; but his ammunition had been expended in the fight, and he had no means of slaying them. His wounds, irritated by the constant exertion in which lay the only hope of life, wore away his strength and at intervals confused his reason. But, even in the wanderings of intellect, Reuben's young heart clung strongly to existence; and it was only through absolute incapacity of motion that he at last sank down beneath a tree, compelled there to await death.

In this situation he was discovered by a party who, upon the first intelligence of the fight, had been despatched to the relief of the survivors. They conveyed him to the nearest settlement, which chanced to be that of his own residence.

Dorcas, in the simplicity of the olden time, watched by the bedside of her wounded lover, and administered all those comforts that are in the sole gift of woman's heart and hand. During several days Reuben's recollection strayed drowsily among the perils and hardships through which he had passed, and he was incapable of returning definite answers to the inquiries with which many were eager to harass him. No authentic particulars of the battle had yet been circulated; nor could mothers, wives, and children tell whether their loved ones were detained by captivity or by the stronger chain of death. Dorcas nourished her apprehensions in silence till one afternoon when Reuben awoke from an unquiet sleep, and seemed to recognize her more perfectly than at any previous time. She saw that his intellect had become composed, and she could no longer restrain her filial anxiety.

"My father, Reuben?" she began; but the change in her lover's countenance made her pause.

The youth shrank as if with a bitter pain, and the blood gushed vividly into his wan and hollow cheeks. His first impulse was to cover his face; but, apparently with a desperate effort, he half raised himself and spoke vehemently, defending himself against an imaginary accusation.

"Your father was sore wounded in the battle, Dorcas; and he bade me not burden myself with him, but only to lead him to the lakeside, that he might quench his thirst and die. But I would not desert the old man in his extremity, and, though bleeding myself, I supported him; I gave him half my strength, and led him away with me. For three days we journeyed on together, and your father was sustained beyond my hopes, but, awaking at sunrise on the fourth day, I found him faint and exhausted; he was unable to proceed; his life had ebbed away fast; and" ——

"He died!" exclaimed Dorcas, faintly.

Reuben felt it impossible to acknowledge that his selfish love of life had hurried him away before her father's fate was decided. He spoke not; he only bowed his head; and, between shame and exhaustion, sank back and hid his face in the pillow. Dorcas wept when her fears were thus confirmed; but the shock, as it had been long anticipated, was on that account the less violent.

"You dug a grave for my poor father in the wilderness, Reuben?" was the question by which her filial piety manifested itself.

"My hands were weak; but I did what I could," replied the youth in a smothered tone. "There stands a noble tombstone above his head; and I would to Heaven I slept as soundly as he!"

Dorcas, perceiving the wildness of his latter words, inquired no further at the time; but her heart found ease in the thought that Roger Malvin had not lacked such funeral rites as it was possible to bestow. The tale of Reuben's courage and fidelity lost nothing when she communicated it to her friends; and the poor youth, tottering from his sick chamber to breathe the sunny air, experienced from every tongue the miserable and humiliating torture of unmerited praise. All acknowledged that he might worthily demand the hand of the fair maiden to whose father he had been "faithful unto death," and, as my tale is not of love, it shall suffice to say that in the space of a few months Reuben became the husband of Dorcas Malvin. During the marriage ceremony the bride was covered with blushes, but the bridegroom's face was pale.

There was now in the breast of Reuben Bourne an incommunicable thought — something which he was to conceal most heedfully from her whom he most loved and trusted. He regretted, deeply and bitterly, the moral cowardice that had restrained his words when he was about to disclose the truth to Dorcas; but pride, the fear of losing her affection, the dread of universal scorn, forbade him to rectify this falsehood. He felt that for leaving Roger Malvin he deserved no censure. His presence, the gratuitous sacrifice of his own life, would have added only another and a needless agony to the last moments of the dying man; but concealment had imparted to a justifiable act much of the secret effect of guilt; and Reuben, while reason told him that he had done right, experienced in no small degree the mental horrors which punish the perpetrator of undiscovered crime. By a certain association of ideas, he at times almost imagined himself a murderer. For years, also, a thought would occasionally recur, which, though he perceived all its folly and extravagance, he had not power to banish from his mind. It was a haunting and torturing fancy that his father-in-law was yet sitting at the foot of the rock, on the withered forest leaves, alive, and awaiting his pledged assistance. These mental deceptions, however, came and went, nor did he ever mistake them for realities; but in the calmest and clearest moods of his mind he was conscious that he had a deep vow unredeemed,

and that an unburied corpse was calling to him
out of the wilderness. Yet such was the consequence of his prevarication that he could not
obey the call. It was now too late to require the
assistance of Roger Malvin's friends in performing his long-deferred sepulture; and superstitious fears, of which none were more susceptible
than the people of the outward settlements,
forbade Reuben to go alone. Neither did he
know where in the pathless and illimitable forest to seek that smooth and lettered rock at the
base of which the body lay: his remembrance
of every portion of his travel thence was indistinct, and the latter part had left no impression
upon his mind. There was, however, a continual impulse, a voice audible only to himself, com-
manding him to go forth and redeem his vow;
and he had a strange impression that, were he
to make the trial, he would be led straight to
Malvin's bones. But year after year that summons, unheard but felt, was disobeyed. His one
secret thought became like a chain binding down
his spirit and like a serpent gnawing into his
heart; and he was transformed into a sad and
downcast yet irritable man.

In the course of a few years after their marriage changes began to be visible in the external
prosperity of Reuben and Dorcas. The only
riches of the former had been his stout heart and
strong arm; but the latter, her father's sole heir-
ess, had made her husband master of a farm,
under older cultivation, larger, and better
stocked than most of the frontier establishments.
Reuben Bourne, however, was a neglectful hus-

bandman; and, while the lands of the other settlers became annually more fruitful, his deteri-
orated in the same proportion. The discourage-
ments to agriculture were greatly lessened by the
cessation of Indian war, during which men held
the plough in one hand and the musket in the
other, and were fortunate if the products of
their dangerous labor were not destroyed, either
in the field or in the barn, by the savage enemy.
But Reuben did not profit by the altered condition of the country; nor can it be denied that his
intervals of industrious attention to his affairs
were but scantily rewarded with success. The irritability by which he had recently become distinguished was another cause of his declining
prosperity, as it occasioned frequent quarrels in
his unavoidable intercourse with the neighboring settlers. The results of these were innumerable lawsuits; for the people of New England, in the earliest stages and wildest circumstances of the country, adopted, whenever attain-
able, the legal mode of deciding their differences. To be brief, the world did not go well
with Reuben Bourne; and, though not till many
years after his marriage, he was finally a ruined
man, with but one remaining expedient against
the evil fate that had pursued him. He was to
throw sunlight into some deep recess of the
forest, and seek subsistence from the virgin
bosom of the wilderness.

The only child of Reuben and Dorcas was
a son, now arrived at the age of fifteen years,
beautiful in youth, and giving promise of a glorious manhood. He was peculiarly qualified for,

and already began to excel in, the wild accomplishments of frontier life. His foot was fleet, his aim true, his apprehension quick, his heart glad and high; and all who anticipated the return of Indian war spoke of Cyrus Bourne as a future leader in the land. The boy was loved by his father with a deep and silent strength as if whatever was good and happy in his own nature had been transferred to his child, carrying his affections with it. Even Dorcas, though loving and beloved, was far less dear to him; for Reuben's secret thoughts and insulated emotions had gradually made him a selfish man, and he could no longer love deeply except where he saw or imagined some reflection or likeness of his own mind. In Cyrus he recognized what he had himself been in other days; and at intervals he seemed to partake of the boy's spirit, and to be revived with a fresh and happy life. Reuben was accompanied by his son in the expedition, for the purpose of selecting a tract of land and felling and burning the timber, which necessarily preceded the removal of the household goods. Two months of autumn were thus occupied, after which Reuben Bourne and his young hunter returned to spend their last winter in the settlements.

It was early in the month of May that the little family snapped asunder whatever tendrils of affections had clung to inanimate objects, and bade farewell to the few who, in the blight of fortune, called themselves their friends. The sadness of the parting moment had, to each of the pilgrims, its peculiar alleviations. Reuben, a moody man, and misanthropic because unhappy, strode onward with his usual stern brow and downcast eye, feeling few regrets and disdaining to acknowledge any. Dorcas, while she wept abundantly over the broken ties by which her simple and affectionate nature had bound itself to everything, felt that the inhabitants of her inmost heart moved on with her, and that all else would be supplied wherever she might go. And the boy dashed one teardrop from his eye, and thought of the adventurous pleasures of the untrodden forest.

Oh, who, in the enthusiasm of a daydream, has not wished that he were a wanderer in a world of summer wilderness, with one fair and gentle being hanging lightly on his arm? In youth his free and exulting step would know no barrier but the rolling ocean or the snow-topped mountains; calmer manhood would choose a home where Nature had strewn a double wealth in the vale of some transparent stream; and when hoary age, after long, long years of that pure life, stole on and found him there, it would find him the father of a race, the patriarch of a people, the founder of a mighty nation yet to be. When death, like the sweet sleep which we welcome after a day of happiness, came over him, his far descendants would mourn over the venerated dust. Enveloped by tradition in mysterious attributes, the men of future generations would call him godlike; and remote posterity would see him standing, dimly glorious, far up the valley of a hundred centuries.

The tangled and gloomy forest through which the personages of my tale were wandering differed widely from the dreamer's land of fantasy; yet there was something in their way of life that Nature asserted as her own, and the gnawing cares which went with them from the world were all that now obstructed their happiness. One stout and shaggy steed, the bearer of all their wealth, did not shrink from the added weight of Dorcas; although her hardy breeding sustained her, during the latter part of each day's journey, by her husband's side. Reuben and his son, their muskets on their shoulders and their axes slung behind them, kept an unwearied pace, each watching with a hunter's eye for the game that supplied their food. When hunger bade, they halted and prepared their meal on the bank of some unpolluted forest brook, which, as they knelt down with thirsty lips to drink, murmured a sweet unwillingness, like a maiden at love's first kiss. They slept beneath a hut of branches, and awoke at peep of light refreshed for the toils of another day. Dorcas and the boy went on joyously, and even Reuben's spirit shone at intervals with an outward gladness; but inwardly there was a cold, cold sorrow, which he compared to the snowdrifts lying deep in the glens and hollows of the rivulets while the leaves were brightly green above.

Cyrus Bourne was sufficiently skilled in the travel of the woods to observe that his father did not adhere to the course they had pursued in their expedition of the preceding autumn. They were now keeping farther to the north, striking out more directly from the settlements, and into a region of which savage beasts and savage men were as yet the sole possessors. The boy sometimes hinted his opinions upon the subject, and Reuben listened attentively, and once or twice altered the direction of their march in accordance with his son's counsel; but, having so done, he seemed ill at ease. His quick and wandering glances were sent forward, apparently in search of enemies lurking behind the tree trunks; and, seeing nothing there, he would cast his eyes backward as if in fear of some pursuer. Cyrus, perceiving that his father gradually resumed the old direction, forbore to interfere; nor, though something began to weigh upon his heart, did his adventurous nature permit him to regret the increased length and the mystery of their way.

On the afternoon of the fifth day they halted, and made their simple encampment nearly an hour before sunset. The face of the country, for the last few miles, had been diversified by swells of land resembling huge waves of a petrified sea; and in one of the corresponding hollows, a wild and romantic spot, had the family reared their hut and kindled their fire. There is something chilling, and yet heartwarming, in the thought of these three, united by strong bands of love and insulated from all that breathe beside. The dark and gloomy pines looked down upon them, and, as the wind swept through their tops, a pitying sound was heard in the forest; or did those old trees groan in fear that men were come to lay the axe to their roots at last? Reuben and his

son, while Dorcas made ready their meal, proposed to wander out in search of game, of
which that day's march had afforded no supply.
The boy, promising not to quit the vicinity of
the encampment, bounded off with a step as
light and elastic as that of the deer he hoped to
slay; while his father, feeling a transient happiness as he gazed after him, was about to pursue
an opposite direction. Dorcas, in the meanwhile,
had seated herself near their fire of fallen
branches, upon the mossgrown and mouldering
trunk of a tree uprooted years before. Her em-
ployment, diversified by an occasional glance
at the pot, now beginning to simmer over the
blaze, was the perusal of the current year's Massachusetts Almanac, which, with the exception of
an old black-letter Bible, comprised all the literary wealth of the family. None pay a greater
regard to arbitrary divisions of time than those
who are excluded from society; and Dorcas mentioned, as if the information were of importance, that it was now the twelfth of May. Her
husband started.

"The twelfth of May! I should remember it
well," muttered he, while many thoughts occasioned a momentary confusion in his mind.
"Where am I? Whither am I wandering? Where
did I leave him?"

Dorcas, too well accustomed to her husband's
wayward moods to note any peculiarity of de-
meanor, now laid aside the almanac and addressed him in that mournful tone which the
tenderhearted appropriate to griefs long cold
and dead.

"It was near this time of the month, eighteen years ago, that my poor father left this world for a better. He had a kind arm to hold his head and a kind voice to cheer him, Reuben, in his last moments; and the thought of the faithful care you took of him has comforted me many a time since. Oh, death would have been awful to a solitary man in a wild place like this!"

"Pray Heaven, Dorcas," said Reuben, in a broken voice, "pray Heaven that neither of us three dies solitary and lies unburied in this howling wilderness!" And he hastened away, leaving her to watch the fire beneath the gloomy pines.

Reuben Bourne's rapid pace gradually slackened as the pang, unintentionally inflicted by the words of Dorcas, became less acute. Many strange reflections, however, thronged upon him; and, straying onward rather like a sleep walker than a hunter, it was attributable to no care of his own that his devious course kept him in the vicinity of the encampment. His steps were imperceptibly led almost in a circle; nor did he observe that he was on the verge of a tract of land heavily timbered, but not with pine trees. The place of the latter was here supplied by oaks and other of the harder woods; and around their roots clustered a dense and bushy undergrowth, leaving, however, barren spaces between the trees, thick strewn with withered leaves. Whenever the rustling of the branches or the creaking of the trunks made a sound, as if the forest were waking from slumber, Reuben instinctively raised the musket that rested on his arm, and cast a quick, sharp glance on every side; but, convinced by a partial observation that no animal was near, he would again give himself up to his thoughts. He was musing on the strange influence that had led him away from his premeditated course, and so far into the depths of the wilderness. Unable to penetrate to the secret place of his soul where his motives lay hidden, he believed that a supernatural voice had called him onward, and that a supernatural power had obstructed his retreat. He trusted that it was Heaven's intent to afford him an opportunity of expiating his sin; he hoped that he might find the bones so long unburied; and that, having laid the earth over them, peace would throw its sunlight into the sepulchre of his heart. From these thoughts he was aroused by a rustling in the forest at some distance from the spot to which he had wandered. Perceiving the motion of some object behind a thick veil of undergrowth, he fired, with the instinct of a hunter and the aim of a practised marksman. A low moan, which told his success, and by which even animals can express their dying agony, was unheeded by Reuben Bourne. What were the recollections now breaking upon him?

The thicket into which Reuben had fired was near the summit of a swell of land, and was clustered around the base of a rock, which, in the shape and smoothness of one of its surfaces, was not unlike a gigantic gravestone. As if reflected in a mirror, its likeness was in Reuben's memory. He even recognized the veins which seemed

to form an inscription in forgotten characters:
everything remained the same, except that a
thick covert of bushes shrouded the lower part
of the rock, and would have hidden Roger Malvin had he still been sitting there. Yet in the
next moment Reuben's eye was caught by another change that time had effected since he
last stood where he was now standing again behind the earthy roots of the uptorn tree. The
sapling to which he had bound the bloodstained
symbol of his vow had increased and strengthened into an oak, far indeed from its maturity,
but with no mean spread of shadowy branches.
There was one singularity observable in this
tree which made Reuben tremble. The middle
and lower branches were in luxuriant life, and
an excess of vegetation had fringed the trunk
almost to the ground; but a blight had apparently stricken the upper part of the oak, and the
very topmost bough was withered, sapless, and
utterly dead. Reuben remembered how the little banner had fluttered on that topmost bough,
when it was green and lovely, eighteen years before. Whose guilt had blasted it?

Dorcas, after the departure of the two hunt-
ers, continued her preparations for their evening
repast. Her sylvan table was the moss-covered
trunk of a large fallen tree, on the broadest
part of which she had spread a snowwhite cloth
and arranged what were left of the bright pew-
ter vessels that had been her pride in the settlements. It had a strange aspect, that one little
spot of homely comfort in the desolate heart of

Nature. The sunshine yet lingered upon the higher branches of the trees that grew on rising ground; but the shadows of evening had deepened into the hollow where the encampment was made, and the firelight began to redden as it gleamed up the tall trunks of the pines or hovered on the dense and obscure mass of foliage that circled round the spot. The heart of Dorcas was not sad; for she felt that it was better to journey in the wilderness with two whom she loved than to be a lonely woman in a crowd that cared not for her. As she busied herself in arranging seats of mouldering wood, covered with leaves, for Reuben and her son, her voice danced through the gloomy forest in the measure of a song that she had learned in youth. The rude melody, the production of a bard who won no name, was descriptive of a winter evening in a frontier cottage, when, secured from savage inroad by the high-piled snowdrifts, the family rejoiced by their own fireside. The whole song possessed the nameless charm peculiar to unborrowed thought, but four continually recurring lines shone out from the rest like the blaze of the hearth whose joys they celebrated. Into them, working magic with a few simple words, the poet had instilled the very essence of domestic love and household happiness, and they were poetry and picture joined in one. As Dorcas sang, the walls of her forsaken home seemed to encircle her; she no longer saw the gloomy pines, nor heard the wind which still, as she began each verse, sent a heavy breath through the branches, and died away in a hollow moan from the bur-

den of the song. She was aroused by the report
of a gun in the vicinity of the encampment; and
either the sudden sound, or her loneliness by the
glowing fire, caused her to tremble violently. The
next moment she laughed in the pride of a
mother's heart.

"My beautiful young hunter! My boy has
slain a deer!" she exclaimed, recollecting that
in the direction whence the shot proceeded Cyrus had gone to the chase.

She waited a reasonable time to hear her son's
light step bounding over the rustling leaves to
tell of his success. But he did not immediately
appear; and she sent her cheerful voice among
the trees in search of him.

"Cyrus! Cyrus!"

His coming was still delayed; and she determined, as the report had apparently been very
near, to seek for him in person. Her assistance,
also, might be necessary in bringing home the
venison which she flattered herself he had obtained. She therefore set forward, directing her
steps by the long-past sound, and singing as she
went, in order that the boy might be aware of
her approach and run to meet her. From behind
the trunk of every tree, and from every hiding
place in the thick foliage of the undergrowth,
she hoped to discover the countenance of her
son, laughing with the sportive mischief that is
born of affection. The sun was now beneath the
horizon, and the light that came down among
the leaves was sufficiently dim to create many
illusions in her expecting fancy. Several times
she seemed indistinctly to see his face gazing out

from among the leaves; and once she imagined that he stood beckoning to her at the base of a craggy rock. Keeping her eyes on this object, however, it proved to be no more than the trunk of an oak fringed to the very ground with little branches, one of which, thrust out farther than the rest, was shaken by the breeze. Making her way round the foot of the rock, she suddenly found herself close to her husband, who had approached in another direction. Leaning upon the butt of his gun, the muzzle of which rested upon the withered leaves, he was apparently absorbed in the contemplation of some object at his feet.

"How is this, Reuben? Have you slain the deer and fallen asleep over him?" exclaimed Dorcas, laughing cheerfully, on her first slight observation of his posture and appearance.

He stirred not, neither did he turn his eyes toward her; and a cold, shuddering fear, indefinite in its source and object, began to creep into her blood. She now perceived that her husband's face was ghastly pale, and his features were rigid, as if incapable of assuming any other expression than the strong despair which had hardened upon them. He gave not the slightest evidence that he was aware of her approach.

"For the love of Heaven, Reuben, speak to me!" cried Dorcas; and the strange sound of her own voice affrighted her even more than the dead silence.

Her husband started, stared into her face,

drew her to the front of the rock, and pointed with his finger.

Oh, there lay the boy, asleep, but dreamless, upon the fallen forest leaves! His cheek rested upon his arm — his curled locks were thrown back from his brow — his limbs were slightly relaxed. Had a sudden weariness overcome the youthful hunter? Would his mother's voice arouse him? She knew that it was death.

"This broad rock is the gravestone of your near kindred, Dorcas," said her husband. "Your tears will fall at once over your father and your son."

She heard him not. With one wild shriek, that seemed to force its way from the sufferer's inmost soul, she sank insensible by the side of her dead boy. At that moment the withered topmost bough of the oak loosened itself in the stilly air, and fell in soft, light fragments upon the rock, upon the leaves, upon Reuben, upon his wife and child, and upon Roger Malvin's bones. Then Reuben's heart was stricken, and the tears gushed out like water from a rock. The vow that the wounded youth had made, the blighted man had come to redeem. His sin was expiated — the curse was gone from him; and in the hour when he had shed blood dearer to him than his own, a prayer, the first for years, went up to Heaven from the lips of Reuben Bourne.

MY KINSMAN, MAJOR MOLINEUX

AFTER THE KINGS of Great Britain had assumed the right of appointing the colonial governors, the measures of the latter seldom met with the ready and generous approbation which had been paid to those of their predecessors, under the original charters. The people looked with most jealous scrutiny to the exercise of power which did not emanate from themselves, and they usually rewarded their rulers with slender gratitude for the compliances by which, in softening their instructions from beyond the sea, they had incurred the reprehension of those who gave them. The annals of Massachusetts Bay will inform us, that of six governors in the space of about forty years from the surrender of the old charter, under James II, two were imprisoned by a popular insurrection; a third, as Hutchinson inclines to believe, was driven from the province by the whizzing of a musket-ball; a fourth, in the opinion of the same historian, was hastened to his grave by continual bickerings with the House of Representatives; and the remaining two, as well as their successors, till the Revolution, were favored with few and brief intervals of peaceful sway. The inferior members of the court party, in times of high political excitement, led scarcely a more desirable life. These remarks may serve as a preface to the following adventures, which chanced upon a summer night, not far from a hundred years ago. The reader, in order to avoid a long and dry detail of colonial affairs, is requested to dispense with an account of the train of circumstances that had caused much temporary inflammation of the popular mind.

It was near nine o'clock of a moonlight evening, when a boat crossed the ferry with a single passenger, who had obtained his conveyance at that unusual hour by the promise of an extra fare. While he stood on the landing place, searching in either pocket for the means of fulfilling his agreement, the ferryman lifted a lantern, by the aid of which, and the newly risen moon, he took a very accurate survey of the stranger's figure. He was a youth of barely eighteen years, evidently country-bred, and now, as it should seem, upon his first visit to town. He was clad in a coarse gray coat, well worn, but in excellent repair; his under garments were durably constructed of leather, and fitted tight to a pair of serviceable and well-shaped limbs;

his stockings of blue yarn were the incontrovertible work of a mother or a sister; and on his head was a three-cornered hat, which in its better days had perhaps sheltered the graver brow of the lad's father. Under his left arm was a heavy cudgel formed of an oak sapling, and retaining a part of the hardened root; and his equipment was completed by a wallet, not so abundantly stocked as to incommode the vigorous shoulders on which it hung. Brown, curly hair, well-shaped features, and bright, cheerful eyes were nature's gifts, and worth all that art could have done for his adornment.

The youth, one of whose names was Robin, finally drew from his pocket the half of a little province bill of five shillings, which, in the depreciation in that sort of currency, did but satisfy the ferryman's demand, with the surplus of a sexangular piece of parchment, valued at three pence. He then walked forward into the town, with as light a step as if his day's journey had not already exceeded thirty miles, and with as eager an eye as if he were entering London city, instead of the little metropolis of a New England colony. Before Robin had proceeded far, however, it occurred to him that he knew not whither to direct his steps; so he paused, and looked up and down the narrow street, scrutinizing the small and mean wooden buildings that were scattered on either side.

"This low hovel cannot be my kinsman's dwelling," thought he, "nor yonder old house, where the moonlight enters at the broken casement; and truly I see none hereabouts that might be worthy of him. It would have been wise to inquire my way of the ferryman, and doubtless he would have gone with me, and earned a shilling from the Major for his pains. But the next man I meet will do as well."

He resumed his walk, and was glad to perceive that the street now became wider, and the houses more respectable in their appearance. He soon discerned a figure moving on moderately in advance, and hastened his steps to overtake it. As Robin drew nigh, he saw that the passenger was a man in years, with a full periwig of gray hair, a wide-skirted coat of dark cloth, and silk stockings rolled above his knees. He carried a long and polished cane, which he struck down perpendicularly before him at every step; and at regular intervals he uttered two successive hems, of a peculiarly solemn and sepulchral intonation. Having made these observations, Robin laid hold of the skirt of the old man's coat, just when the light from the open door and windows of a barber's shop fell upon both their figures.

"Good evening to you, honored sir," said he, making a low bow, and still retaining his hold of the skirt. "I pray you tell me whereabouts is the dwelling of my kinsman, Major Molineux."

The youth's question was uttered very loudly; and one of the barbers, whose razor was descending on a well-soaped chin, and another who was dressing a Ramillies wig, left their occupations, and came to the door. The citizen, in the mean time, turned a long-favored countenance upon Robin, and answered him in a tone of excessive anger and annoyance. His two sepulchral hems, however, broke into the very center of his rebuke, with most singular effect, like a thought of the cold grave obtruding among wrathful passions.

"Let go my garment, fellow! I tell you, I know not the man you speak of. What! I have authority, I have — hem, hem — authority; and if this be the respect you show for your betters, your feet shall be brought acquainted with the stocks by daylight, tomorrow morning!"

Robin released the old man's skirt, and hastened away, pursued by an ill-mannered roar of laughter from the barber's shop. He was at first considerably surprised by the result of his question, but, being a shrewd youth, soon thought himself able to account for the mystery.

"This is some country representative," was his conclusion, "who has never seen the inside of my kinsman's door, and lacks the breeding to answer a stranger civilly. The man is old, or verily — I might be tempted to turn back and smite him on the nose. Ah, Robin, Robin! even the barber's boys laugh at you for choosing such a guide! You will be wiser in time, friend Robin."

He now became entangled in a succession of crooked and narrow streets, which crossed each other, and meandered at no great distance from the waterside. The smell of tar was obvious to his nostrils, the masts of vessels pierced the moonlight above the tops of the buildings, and the numerous signs, which Robin paused to read, informed him that he was near the center of business. But the streets were empty, the shops were closed, and lights were visible only in the second stories of a few dwelling houses. At length, on the corner of a narrow lane, through which he was passing, he beheld the broad countenance of a British hero swinging before the door of an inn, whence proceeded the voices of many guests. The casement of one of the lower windows was thrown back, and a very thin curtain permitted Robin to distinguish a party at supper, round a well-furnished table. The fragrance of the good cheer steamed forth into the outer air, and the youth could not fail to recollect that the last remnant of his traveling stock of provision had yielded to his morning appetite, and that noon had found and left him dinnerless.

"Oh, that a parchment three-penny might give me a right to sit down at yonder table!" said Robin, with a sigh. "But the Major will make me welcome to the best of his victuals; so I will even step boldly in, and inquire my way to his dwelling."

He entered the tavern, and was guided by the murmur of voices and the fumes of tobacco to the public room. It was a long and low apartment, with oaken walls, grown dark in the continual smoke, and a floor which was thickly sanded, but of no immaculate purity. A number of persons — the larger part of whom appeared to be mariners, or in some way connected with the sea — occupied the wooden benches, or leather-bottomed chairs, conversing on various matters, and occasionally lending their attention to some topic of general interest. Three or

four little groups were draining as many bowls
of punch, which the West India trade had long
since made a familiar drink in the colony. Others, who had the appearance of men who lived
by regular and laborious handicraft, preferred
the insulated bliss of an unshared potation, and
became more taciturn under its influence.
Nearly all, in short, evinced a predilection for
the Good Creature in some of its various
shapes, for this is a vice to which, as Fast Day
sermons of a hundred years ago will testify, we
have a long hereditary claim. The only guests
to whom Robin's sympathies inclined him were
two or three sheepish countrymen, who were
using the inn somewhat after the fashion of a
Turkish caravansary; they had gotten themselves
into the darkest corner of the room, and heed-
less of the Nicotian atmosphere, were supping
on the bread of their own ovens, and the ba-
con cured in their own chimney smoke. But
though Robin felt a sort of brotherhood with
these strangers, his eyes were attracted from
them to a person who stood near the door, holding whispered conversation with a group of ill-
dressed associates. His features were separately
striking almost to grotesqueness, and the whole
face left a deep impression on the memory. The
forehead bulged out into a double prominence, with a vale between; the nose came
boldly forth in an irregular curve, and its bridge
was of more than a finger's breadth; the eyebrows were deep and shaggy, and the eyes
glowed beneath them like fire in a cave.

While Robin deliberated of whom to inquire

respecting his kinsman's dwelling, he was accosted by the innkeeper, a little man in a stained white apron, who had come to pay his professional welcome to the stranger. Being in the second generation from a French Protestant, he seemed to have inherited the courtesy of his parent nation; but no variety of circumstances was ever known to change his voice from the one shrill note in which he now addressed Robin.

"From the country, I presume, sir?" said he, with a profound bow. "Beg leave to congratulate you on your arrival, and trust you intend a long stay with us. Fine town here, sir, beautiful buildings, and much that may interest a stranger. May I hope for the honor of your commands in respect to supper?"

"The man sees a family likeness! the rogue has guessed that I am related to the Major!" thought Robin, who had hitherto experienced little superfluous civility.

All eyes were now turned on the country lad, standing at the door, in his worn three-cornered hat, gray coat, leather breeches, and blue yarn stockings, leaning on an oaken cudgel, and bearing a wallet on his back.

Robin replied to the courteous innkeeper, with such an assumption of confidence as befitted the Major's relative. "My honest friend," he said, "I shall make it a point to patronize your house on some occasion, when" — here he could not help lowering his voice — "when I may have more than a parchment three pence in my pocket. My present business," continued he, speaking with lofty confidence, "is merely to inquire my way to the dwelling of my kinsman, Major Molineux."

There was a sudden and general movement in the room, which Robin interpreted as expressing the eagerness of each individual to become his guide. But the innkeeper turned his eyes to a written paper on the wall, which he read, or seemed to read, with occasional recurrences to the young man's figure.

"What have we here?" said he, breaking his speech into little dry fragments. " 'Left the house of the subscriber, bounden servant, Hezekiah Mudge — had on, when he went away, gray coat, leather breeches, master's third-best hat. One pound currency reward to whosoever shall lodge him in any jail of the providence.' Better trudge, boy; better trudge!"

Robin had begun to draw his hand toward the lighter end of the oak cudgel, but a strange hostility in every countenance induced him to relinquish his purpose of breaking the courteous innkeeper's head. As he turned to leave the room, he encountered a sneering glance from the bold-featured personage whom he had before noticed; and no sooner was he beyond the door, than he heard a general laugh, in which the innkeeper's voice might be distinguished, like the dropping of small stones into a kettle.

"Now, is it not strange," thought Robin, with his usual shrewdness, "is it not strange that the confession of an empty pocket should outweigh the name of my kinsman, Major Molineux? Oh, if I had one of those grinning rascals in the woods, where I and my oak sapling grew up together, I would teach him that my arm is heavy though my purse be light!"

On turning the corner of the narrow lane, Robin found himself in a spacious street, with an unbroken line of lofty houses on each side, and a steepled building at the upper end, whence the ringing of a bell announced the hour of nine. The light of the moon, and the lamps from the numerous shopwindows, discovered people promenading on the pavement, and amongst them Robin had hoped to recognize his hitherto inscrutable relative. The result of his former inquiries made him unwilling to hazard another, in a scene of such publicity, and he determined to walk slowly and silently up the street, thrusting his face close to that of every elderly gentleman, in search of the Major's lineaments. In his progress, Robin encountered many gay and gallant figures. Embroidered garments of showy colors, enormous periwigs, gold-laced hats, and silver-hilted swords glided past him and dazzled his optics. Traveled youths, imitators of the European fine gentlemen of the period, trod jauntily along, half dancing to the fashionable tunes which they hummed, and making poor Robin ashamed of his quiet and natural gait. At length, after many pauses to examine the gorgeous display of goods in the shopwindows, and after suffering some rebukes for the impertinence of his scrutiny into people's faces, the Major's kinsman found himself near the steepled building, still unsuccessful in his search. As yet, however, he had seen only one side of the thronged street; so

Robin crossed, and continued the same sort of inquisition down the opposite pavement, with stronger hopes than the philosopher seeking an honest man, but with no better fortune. He had arrived about midway toward the lower end, from which his course began, when he overheard the approach of someone who struck down a cane on the flag-stones at every step, uttering at regular intervals, two sepulchral hems.

"Mercy on us!" quoth Robin, recognizing the sound.

Turning a corner, which chanced to be close at his right hand, he hastened to pursue his researches in some other part of the town. His patience now was wearing low, and he seemed to feel more fatigue from his rambles since he crossed the ferry, than from his journey of several days on the other side. Hunger also pleaded loudly within him, and Robin began to balance the propriety of demanding, violently, and with lifted cudgel, the necessary guidance from the first solitary passenger whom he should meet. While a resolution to this effect was gaining strength, he entered a street of mean appearance, on either side of which a row of ill-built houses was straggling toward the harbor. The moonlight fell upon no passenger along the whole extent, but in the third domicile which Robin passed there was a half-opened door, and his keen glance detected a woman's garment within.

"My luck may be better here," said he to himself.

Accordingly, he approached the door and beheld it shut closer as he did so; yet an open space remained, sufficing for the fair occupant to observe the stranger, without a corresponding display on her part. All that Robin could discern was a strip of scarlet petticoat, and the occasional sparkle of an eye, as if the moonbeams were trembling on some bright thing.

"Pretty mistress," for I may call her so with a good conscience, thought the shrewd youth, since I know nothing to the contrary, "my sweet pretty mistress, will you be kind enough to tell me whereabouts I must seek the dwelling of my kinsman, Major Molineux?"

Robin's voice was plaintive and winning, and the female, seeing nothing to be shunned in the handsome country youth, thrust open the door, and came forth into the moonlight. She was a dainty little figure, with a white neck, round arms, and a slender waist, at the extremity of which her scarlet petticoat jutted out over a hoop, as if she were standing on a balloon. Moreover, her face was oval and pretty, her hair dark beneath the little cap, and her bright eyes possessed a sly freedom, which triumphed over those of Robin.

"Major Molineux dwells here," said this fair woman.

Now, her voice was the sweetest Robin had heard that night, yet he could not help doubting whether that sweet voice spoke Gospel truth. He looked up and down the mean street, and then surveyed the house before which they stood. It was a small, dark edifice of two stories, the second of which projected over the lower floor, and the front apartment had the aspect of a shop for petty commodities.

"Now, truly, I am in luck," replied Robin, cunningly, "and so indeed is my kinsman, the Major, in having so pretty a housekeeper. But I prithee trouble him to step to the door; I will deliver him a message from his friends in the country, and then go back to my lodgings at the inn."

"Nay, the Major has been abed this hour or more," said the lady of the scarlet petticoat, "and it would be to little purpose to disturb him tonight, seeing his evening draught was of the strongest. But he is a kindhearted man, and it would be as much as my life's worth to let a kinsman of his turn away from the door. You are the good old gentleman's very picture, and I could swear that was his rainy-weather hat. Also he has garments very much resembling those leather smallclothes. But come in, I pray, for I bid you hearty welcome in his name."

So saying, the fair and hospitable dame took our hero by the hand; and the touch was light, and the force was gentleness, and though Robin read in her eyes what he did not hear in her words, yet the slender-waisted woman in the scarlet petticoat proved stronger than the athletic country youth. She had drawn his half-willing footsteps nearly to the threshold, when the opening of a door in the neighborhood startled the Major's housekeeper, and, leaving the Major's kinsman, she vanished speedily into her own domicile. A heavy yawn preceded the appearance of a man, who, like the Moonshine of Pyramus and Thisbe, carried a lantern, needlessly aiding his sister luminary in the heavens. As he walked sleepily up the street, he turned his broad, dull face on Robin, and displayed a long staff, spiked at the end.

"Home, vagabond, home!" said the watchman, in accents that seemed to fall asleep as soon as they were uttered. "Home, or we'll set you in the stocks by peep of day!"

"This is the second hint of the kind," thought Robin. "I wish they would end my difficulties, by setting me there tonight."

Nevertheless, the youth felt an instinctive antipathy toward the guardian of midnight order, which at first prevented him from asking his usual question. But just when the man was about to vanish behind the corner, Robin resolved not to lose the opportunity, and shouted lustily after him,

"I say, friend! will you guide me to the house of my kinsman, Major Molineux?"

The watchman made no reply, but turned the corner and was gone; yet Robin seemed to hear the sound of drowsy laughter stealing along the solitary street. At that moment, also, a pleasant titter saluted him from the open window above his head; he looked up, and caught the sparkle of a saucy eye; a round arm beckoned to him, and next he heard light footsteps descending the staircase within. But Robin, being of the household of a New England clergyman, was a good youth, as well as a shrewd one; so he resisted temptation, and fled away.

He now roamed desperately, and at random, through the town, almost ready to believe that a spell was on him, like that by which a wizard of his country had once kept three pursuers wandering, a whole winter night, within twenty paces of the cottage which they sought. The streets lay before him, strange and desolate, and the lights were extinguished in almost every house. Twice, however, little parties of men, among whom Robin distinguished individuals in outlandish attire, came hurrying along; but, though on both occasions, they paused to address him, such intercourse did not at all enlighten his perplexity. They did but utter a few words in some language of which Robin knew nothing, and perceiving his inability to answer, bestowed a curse upon him in plain English and hastened away. Finally, the lad determined to knock at the door of every mansion that might appear worthy to be occupied by his kinsman, trusting that perseverance would overcome the fatality that had hitherto thwarted him. Firm in this resolve, he was passing beneath the walls of a church, which formed the corner of two streets, when, as he turned into the shade of its steeple, he encountered a bulky stranger, muffled in a cloak. The man was proceeding with the speed of earnest business, but Robin planted himself full before him, holding the oak cudgel with both hands across his body as a bar to further passage.

"Halt, honest man, and answer me a question," said he, very resolutely. "Tell me, this

instant, whereabouts is the dwelling of my kinsman, Major Molineux!"

"Keep your tongue between your teeth, fool,
and let me pass!" said a deep, gruff voice, which
Robin partly remembered. "Let me pass, or I'll
strike you to the earth!"

"No, no, neighbor!" cried Robin, flourishing
his cudgel, and then thrusting its larger end
close to the man's muffled face. "No, no, I'm not
the fool you take me for, nor do you pass till I
have an answer to my question. Whereabouts is
the dwelling of my kinsman, Major Molineux?"

The stranger, instead of attempting to force
his passage, stepped back into the moonlight,
unmuffled his face, and stared full into that of
Robin.

"Watch here an hour, and Major Molineux
will pass by," said he.

Robin gazed with dismay and astonishment
on the unprecedented physiognomy of the
speaker. The forehead with its double prominence, the broad hooked nose, the shaggy eyebrows, and fiery eyes were those which he had
noticed at the inn, but the man's complexion
had undergone a singular, or, more properly, a
twofold change. One side of the face blazed an
intense red, while the other was black as midnight, the division line being in the broad
bridge of the nose; and a mouth which seemed
to extend from ear to ear was black or red, in
contrast to the color of the cheek. The effect was
as if two individual devils, a fiend of fire and a
fiend of darkness, had united themselves to form
this infernal visage. The stranger grinned in

Robin's face, muffled his parti-colored features, and was out of sight in a moment.

"Strange things we travelers see!" ejaculated Robin.

He seated himself, however, upon the steps of the church door, resolving to wait the appointed time for his kinsman. A few moments were consumed in philosophical speculations upon the species of man who had just left him; but having settled this point shrewdly, rationally, and satisfactorily, he was compelled to look elsewhere for his amusement. And first he threw his eyes along the street. It was of more respectable appearance than most of those into which he had wandered; and the moon, creating, like the imaginative power, a beautiful strangeness in familiar objects, gave something of romance to a scene that might not have possessed it in the light of day. The irregular and often quaint architecture of the houses, some of whose roofs were broken into numerous little peaks, while others ascended, steep and narrow, into a single point, and others again were square; the pure snow-white of some of their complexions, the aged darkness of others, and the thousand sparklings, reflected from bright substances in the walls of many; these matters engaged Robin's attention for a while, and then began to grow wearisome. Next he endeavored to define the forms of distant objects, starting away, with almost ghostly indistinctness, just as his eye appeared to grasp them; and finally he took a minute survey of an edifice which stood on the opposite side of the street, directly in front of the

church door, where he was stationed. It was a
large, square mansion, distinguished from its
neighbors by a balcony, which rested on tall
pillars, and by an elaborate Gothic window,
communicating therewith.

"Perhaps this is the very house I have been
seeking," thought Robin.

Then he strove to speed away the time, by
listening to a murmur which swept continually
along the street, yet was scarcely audible, except
to an unaccustomed ear like his; it was a low,
dull, dreamy sound, compounded of many noises,
each of which was at too great a distance to be
separately heard. Robin marveled at this snore
of a sleeping town, and marveled more whenever its continuity was broken by now and then
a distant shout, apparently loud where it orig-
inated. But altogether it was a sleep-inspiring
sound, and, to shake off its drowsy influence,
Robin arose, and climbed a window-frame, that
he might view the interior of the church. There
the moonbeams came trembling in, and fell
down upon the deserted pews, and extended
along the quiet aisles. A fainter yet more awful
radiance was hovering around the pulpit, and
one solitary ray had dared to rest upon the open
page of the great Bible. Had nature, in that
deep hour, become a worshiper in the house
which man had built? Or was that heavenly light
the visible sanctity of the place — visible because no earthly and impure feet were within
the walls? The scene made Robin's heart shiver
with a sensation of loneliness stronger than he
had ever felt in the remotest depths of his na-

tive woods; so he turned away and sat down again before the door. There were graves around the church, and now an uneasy thought obtruded into Robin's breast. What if the object of his search, which had been so often and so strangely thwarted, were all the time moldering in his shroud? What if his kinsman should glide through yonder gate, and nod and smile to him in dimly passing by?

"Oh that any breathing thing were here with me!" said Robin.

Recalling his thoughts from this uncomfortable track, he sent them over forest, hill, and stream, and attempted to imagine how that evening of ambiguity and weariness had been spent by his father's household. He pictured them assembled at the door, beneath the tree, the great old tree, which had been spared for its huge twisted trunk and venerable shade, when a thousand leafy brethren fell. There, at the going down of the summer sun, it was his father's custom to perform domestic worship, that the neighbors might come and join with him like brothers of the family, and that the wayfaring man might pause to drink at that fountain, and keep his heart pure by freshening the memory of home. Robin distinguished the seat of every individual of the little audience; he saw the good man in the midst, holding the Scriptures in the golden light that fell from the western clouds; he beheld him close the book and all rise up to pray. He heard the old thanksgivings for daily mercies, the old supplications for their continuance, to which he had so often listened in weariness, but which were now among his dear remembrances. He perceived the slight inequality of his father's voice when he came to speak of the absent one; he noted how his mother turned her face to the broad and knotted trunk; how his elder brother scorned, because the beard was rough upon his upper lip, to permit his features to be moved; how the younger sister drew down a low hanging branch before her eyes; and how the little one of all, whose sports had hitherto broken the decorum of the scene, understood the prayer for her playmate, and burst into clamorous grief. Then he saw them go in at the door; and when Robin would have entered also, the latch tinkled into its place, and he was excluded from his home.

"Am I here, or there?" cried Robin, starting; for all at once, when his thoughts had become visible and audible in a dream, the long, wide, solitary street shone out before him.

He aroused himself, and endeavored to fix his attention steadily upon the large edifice which he had surveyed before. But still his mind kept vibrating between fancy and reality; by turns, the pillars of the balcony lengthened into the tall, bare stems of pines, dwindled down to human figures, settled again into their true shape and size, and then commenced a new succession of changes. For a single moment, when he deemed himself awake, he could have sworn that a visage — one which he seemed to remember, yet could not absolutely name as his kinsman's — was looking toward him from the Gothic window. A deeper sleep wrestled with and nearly overcame him, but fled at the sound of footsteps along the opposite pavement. Robin rubbed his eyes, discerned a man passing at the foot of the balcony, and addressed him in a loud, peevish, and lamentable cry.

"Hallo, friend! must I wait here all night for my kinsman, Major Molineux?"

The sleeping echoes awoke, and answered the voice; and the passenger, barely able to discern a figure sitting in the oblique shade of the steeple, traversed the street to obtain a nearer view. He was himself a gentleman in his prime, of open, intelligent, cheerful, and altogether prepossessing countenance. Perceiving a country youth, apparently homeless and without friends, he accosted him in a tone of real kindness, which had become strange to Robin's ears.

"Well, my good lad, why are you sitting here?" inquired he. "Can I be of service to you in any way?"

"I am afraid not, sir," replied Robin, despondingly; "yet I shall take it kindly, if you'll answer me a single question. I've been searching, half the night, for one Major Molineux; now, sir, is there really such a person in these parts, or am I dreaming?"

"Major Molineux! The name is not altogether strange to me," said the gentleman, smiling. "Have you any objection to telling me the nature of your business with him?"

Then Robin briefly related that his father was a clergyman, settled on a small salary, at a long distance back in the country, and that he and Major Molineux were brothers' children. The

Major, having inherited riches, and acquired civil and military rank, had visited his cousin, in great pomp, a year or two before; had manifested much interest in Robin and an elder brother, and, being childless himself, had thrown out hints respecting the future establishment of one of them in life. The elder brother was destined to succeed to the farm which his father cultivated in the interval of sacred duties; it was therefore determined that Robin should profit by his kinsman's generous intentions, especially as he seemed to be rather the favorite, and was thought to possess other necessary endowments.

"For I have the name of being a shrewd youth," observed Robin, in this part of his story.

"I doubt not you deserve it," replied his new friend, good-naturedly, "but pray proceed."

"Well, sir, being nearly eighteen years old, and well grown, as you see," continued Robin, drawing himself up to his full height, "I thought it high time to begin in the world. So my mother and sister put me in handsome trim, and my father gave me half the remnant of his last year's salary, and five days ago I started for this place, to pay the Major a visit. But, would you believe it, sir! I crossed the ferry a little after dark, and have yet found nobody that would show me the way to his dwelling; only, an hour or two since, I was told to wait here, and Major Molineux would pass by."

"Can you describe the man who told you this?" inquired the gentleman.

"Oh, he was a very ill-favored fellow, sir,"

replied Robin, "with two great bumps on his forehead, a hook nose, fiery eyes; and, what struck me as the strangest, his face was of two different colors. Do you happen to know such a man, sir?"

"Not intimately," answered the stranger, "but I chanced to meet him a little time previous to your stopping me. I believe you may trust his word, and that the Major will very shortly pass through this street. In the mean time, as I have a singular curiosity to witness your meeting, I will sit down here upon the steps and bear you company."

He seated himself accordingly, and soon engaged his companion in animated discourse. It was but of brief continuance, however, for a noise of shouting, which had long been remotely audible, drew so much nearer that Robin inquired its cause.

"What may be the meaning of this uproar?" asked he. "Truly, if your town be always as noisy, I shall find little sleep while I am an inhabitant."

"Why, indeed, friend Robin, there do appear to be three or four riotous fellows abroad tonight," replied the gentleman. "You must not expect all the stillness of your native woods here in our streets. But the watch will shortly be at the heels of these lads and — "

"Ay, and set them in the stocks by peep of day," interrupted Robin, recollecting his own encounter with the drowsy lantern bearer. "But, dear sir, if I may trust my ears, an army of watchmen would never make head against such a multitude of rioters. There were at least a thousand voices went up to make that one shout."

"May not a man have several voices, Robin, as well as two complexions?" said his friend.

"Perhaps a man may; but Heaven forbid that a woman should!" responded the shrewd youth, thinking of the seductive tones of the Major's housekeeper.

The sounds of a trumpet in some neighboring street now became so evident and continual, that Robin's curiosity was strongly excited. In addition to the shouts, he heard frequent bursts from many instruments of discord, and a wild and confused laughter filled up the intervals. Robin rose from the steps, and looked wistfully toward a point whither people seemed to be hastening.

"Surely some prodigious merry-making is going on," exclaimed he. "I have laughed very little since I left home, sir, and should be sorry to lose an opportunity. Shall we step round the corner by that darkish house, and take our share of the fun?"

"Sit down again, sit down, good Robin," replied the gentleman, laying his hand on the skirt of the gray coat. "You forget that we must wait here for your kinsman; and there is reason to believe that he will pass by, in the course of a very few moments."

The near approach of the uproar had now disturbed the neighborhood; windows flew open on all sides; and many heads, in the attire of the pillow, and confused by sleep suddenly broken, were protruded to the gaze of whoever had lei-

sure to observe them. Eager voices hailed each
other from house to house, all demanding the
explanation, which not a soul could give. Half-
dressed men hurried toward the unknown com-
motion, stumbling as they went over the stone
steps that thrust themselves into the narrow
footwalk. The shouts, the laughter, and the
tuneless bray, the antipodes of music, came onward with increasing din, till scattered individuals, and then denser bodies, began to appear
round a corner at the distance of a hundred
yards.

"Will you recognize your kinsman, if he passes
in this crowd?" inquired the gentleman.

"Indeed, I can't warrant it, sir; but I'll take
my stand here, and keep a bright lookout," answered Robin, descending to the outer edge of
the pavement.

A mighty stream of people now emptied into
the street, and came rolling slowly toward the
church. A single horseman wheeled the corner
in the midst of them, and close behind him
came a band of fearful wind instruments, sending forth a fresher discord now that no interven-
ing buildings kept it from the ear. Then a red-
der light disturbed the moonbeams, and a dense
multitude of torches shone along the street, concealing, by their glare, whatever object they illuminated. The single horseman, clad in a military dress, and bearing a drawn sword, rode
onward as the leader, and, by his fierce and var-
iegated countenance, appeared like war person-
ified; the red of one cheek was an emblem of
fire and sword; the blackness of the other betokened the mourning that attends them. In

his train were wild figures in the Indian dress, and many fantastic shapes without a model, giving the whole march a visionary air, as if a dream had broken forth from some feverish brain, and were sweeping visibly through the midnight streets. A mass of people, inactive, except as applauding spectators, hemmed the procession in; and several women ran along the sidewalk, piercing the confusion of heavier sounds with their shrill voices of mirth or terror.

"The double-faced fellow has his eye upon me," muttered Robin, with an indefinite but an uncomfortable idea that he was himself to bear a part in the pageantry.

The leader turned himself in the saddle, and fixed his glance full upon the country youth, as the steed went slowly by. When Robin had freed his eyes from those fiery ones, the musicians were passing before him, and the torches were close at hand; but the unsteady brightness of the latter formed a veil which he could not penetrate. The rattling of wheels over the stones sometimes found its way to his ear, and confused traces of a human form appeared at intervals, and then melted into the vivid light. A moment more, and the leader thundered a command to halt: the trumpets vomited a horrid breath, and then held their peace; the shouts and laughter of the people died away, and there remained only a universal hum, allied to silence. Right before Robin's eyes was an uncovered cart. There the torches blazed the brightest, there the moon shone out like day, and there, in tar-and-feathery dignity, sat his kinsman, Major Molineux!

He was an elderly man, of large and majestic person, and strong, square features, betokening a steady soul; but steady as it was, his enemies had found means to shake it. His face was pale as death, and far more ghastly; the broad forehead was contracted in his agony, so that his eyebrows formed one grizzled line; his eyes were red and wild, and the foam hung white upon his quivering lip. His whole frame was agitated by a quick and continual tremor, which his pride strove to quell, even in those circumstances of overwhelming humiliation. But perhaps the bitterest pang of all was when his eyes met those of Robin; for he evidently knew him on the instant, as the youth stood witnessing the foul disgrace of a head grown gray in honor. They stared at each other in silence, and Robin's knees shook, and his hair bristled, with a mixture of pity and terror. Soon, however, a bewildering excitement began to seize upon his mind; the preceding adventures of the night, the unexpected appearance of the crowd, the torches, the confused din and the hush that followed, the spectre of his kinsman reviled by that great multitude — all this, and, more than all, a perception of tremendous ridicule in the whole scene, affected him with a sort of mental inebriety. At that moment a voice of sluggish merriment saluted Robin's ears; he turned instinctively, and just behind the corner of the church stood the lantern bearer, rubbing his eyes, and drowsily enjoying the lad's amazement. Then he heard a peal of laughter like the ringing of silvery bells; a woman twitched his arm, a saucy eye met his, and he saw the lady of the scarlet

petticoat. A sharp, dry cachinnation appealed
to his memory, and, standing on tiptoe in the
crowd, with his white apron over his head, he
beheld the courteous little innkeeper. And
lastly, there sailed over the heads of the multitude a great, broad laugh, broken in the midst
by two sepulchral hems; thus, "Haw, haw,
haw — hem, hem — haw, haw, haw, haw!"

The sound proceeded from the balcony of
the opposite edifice, and thither Robin turned
his eyes. In front of the Gothic window stood
the old citizen, wrapped in a wide gown, his
gray periwig exchanged for a nightcap, which
was thrust back from his forehead, and his silk
stockings hanging about his legs. He supported
himself on his polished cane in a fit of convulsive merriment, which manifested itself on his
solemn old features like a funny inscription on
a tombstone. Then Robin seemed to hear the
voices of the barbers, of the guests of the inn,
and of all who had made sport of him that
night. The contagion was spreading among the
multitude, when all at once, it seized upon
Robin, and he sent forth a shout of laughter
that echoed through the street — every man
shook his sides, every man emptied his lungs,
but Robin's shout was the loudest there. The
cloud-spirits peeped from their silvery islands,
as the congregated mirth went roaring up the
sky! The Man in the Moon heard the far bellow.
"Oho," quoth he, "the old earth is frolicsome
tonight!"

When there was a momentary calm in that
tempestuous sea of sound, the leader gave the
sign, the procession resumed its march. On they

went, like fiends that throng in mockery around some dead potentate, mighty no more, but majestic still in his agony. On they went, in counterfeited pomp, in senseless uproar, in frenzied merriment, trampling all on an old man's heart. On swept the tumult, and left a silent street behind.

"Well, Robin, are you dreaming?" inquired the gentleman, laying his hand on the youth's shoulder.

Robin started, and withdrew his arm from the stone post to which he had instinctively clung, as the living stream rolled by him. His cheek was somewhat pale, and his eye not quite as lively as in the earlier part of the evening.

"Will you be kind enough to show me the way to the ferry?" said he, after a moment's pause.

"You have, then, adopted a new subject of inquiry?" observed his companion, with a smile.

"Why, yes, sir," replied Robin, rather dryly. "Thanks to you, and to my other friends, I have at last met my kinsman, and he will scarce desire to see my face again. I begin to grow weary of a town life, sir. Will you show me the way to the ferry?"

"No, my good friend Robin — not tonight, at least," said the gentleman. "Some few days hence, if you wish it, I will speed you on your journey. Or, if you prefer to remain with us, perhaps, as you are a shrewd youth, you may rise in the world without the help of your kinsman, Major Molineux."

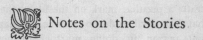 Notes on the Stories

Young Goodman Brown, p. 11

SALEM VILLAGE, in Puritan times, was a somber little farming community ruled very strictly by its elders. It had been founded in 1672 as a parish, separate from the busy seaport of Salem town; and it was known for the "contentious" nature of its inhabitants, who made life so unpleasant for at least two of their ministers that the men of God left town in disgust. In 1689, Reverend Samuel Parris took over the parish and governed it as if the congregation were made up entirely of naughty children. Needless to say, he always had an eye out for evidences of sin.

In 1692, Salem village became the scene of witch trials. Nathaniel Hawthorne's interest in the background of those trials (and in the kind of adventure experienced by young Goodman Brown) was surely stimulated by the fact that his own ancestor, Magistrate John Hathorne, was the man who conducted the examinations of the accused witches and presided at the trials. It must be a strange sensation to discover that one's own ancestor was such a cruel man, a fanatic who was convinced he was a saint. Not surprisingly, Nathaniel Hawthorne brooded a great deal about it; and it may even have had something to do with his changing his last name to "Hawthorne."

There were no juries at the witch trials, and the accused were not presumed innocent until proven guilty. The judges had no laws to consult for "proof," in any case. They relied on the legendary tests for witchcraft: a peculiar mark on the body; the conviction that "the devil could not assume the shape of an innocent person in doing mischief to mankind." ("Mischief" could mean anything from smashing a wagon wheel, gossiping, losing someone's rake, to being nearby when someone's cow was drowned.)

Young Goodman Brown's mysterious adventure takes place a short time before the hysteria about witches began. When you realize how close Salem village was to the forest (where there might be "a devilish Indian behind every tree") you will understand some of the reasons for the villagers' nervousness. Turning in one direction, a person faced the meetinghouse; turning in the other, he faced the wilderness.

The wilderness had signified danger to the early settlers for good reason; and, even in the 1690's, Indian raids were not unknown. But, by this time, the forest was thought of as the breeding ground of everything that was sinful and disorderly — everything that meant relaxation, freedom, and excitement, things which were thought to threaten Puritan control. Indians and wild animals were bad enough. The existence of hidden clearings and of secret meeting places was even worse. Like many rigid, close-minded people, the elders did not trust their fellowmen when they were out of sight. Perhaps because the elders had forbidden wishes of their own, they believed people had to be watched (and know they were being watched) if they were to remain obedient and "good."

Many writers, before and after Hawthorne, have been fascinated by the extremism of these self-appointed saints who spent their time exposing evil. The playwright, Arthur Miller, is one of several contemporary artists who has let his imagination work on Salem village. You may be familiar with his play, *The Crucible,* which is based on what actually happened in Salem in the 1690's. Like Miller, you may be able to see connections between the mass hysteria there and modern instances of fanaticism and persecution. Miller knows, as Hawthorne did, that no human being is perfect, and that human imperfection is no excuse, either for persecution of particular individuals or for losing faith in mankind.

Young Goodman Brown's problem is that he is human. Because he is human — and therefore imperfect — he is tempted by the darkness of the forest, by the "forbidden games" played there at night. He is young, however, and he is not sure of himself. He is called "Goodman" because that was the name for a head of a household, or a husband; but he has only been married for three months. He has "scruples" about the appointment he has made with the worldly gentleman carrying the oddly shaped staff; and, like many young people, he thinks he is the only one who has been tempted to do something he is really afraid to do. In spite of his scruples, and with a guilty promise to be home by sunrise, he leaves his pretty wife with the pink ribbon in her hair. When he meets the older man ("in grave and decent attire"), he tries to back out of the trip he said he would take. Nobody in the Brown family, he insists, can ever have done such a thing; and he is incredulous when he learns that his own father and grandfather have done things much, much worse.

Who is this older man, young Goodman's guide? Can he really be the young man's grandfather? And, if he is, why does he think it so important for Goodman Brown to have this experience in the woods at night? Imagine how you would feel if, when you mentioned your minister ("that good old man" whose very voice would make you feel guilty if you had done wrong), your words were greeted with derisive laughter. Does Goodman see — or think he sees — the old lady who taught him his catechism when he was little? (Her name, by the way, is Goody Cloyse, and a woman named Goody Cloyse was one of the first to be accused of witchcraft in the historic trials.) Does he hear — or think he hears — the voices of the deacon and the minister anticipating a mysterious meeting planned for that very night? Is the uncertain, pleading voice, rising over the chorus of familiar Salem voices, that of his own wife, Faith?

You must decide for yourself; in Hawthorne's imaginary world, there are always two possibilities — the natural and the supernatural. Be sure, though, to let yourself *see* what happens, especially "in the heart of the dark wilderness," with the black pine trees, the red-lit clearing, the blazing foliage around the pinnacle of the rock. Picture what you would see if a camera were moving from face to face in that crowd of Brown's fellow villagers, with each face emerging momentarily as the firelight glances over it. You, too, may be "bedazzled"; but if you are not, there will be no puzzle, no sense of mystery.

The last section, which describes the morning after, holds a buried moral. Perhaps it does not matter if the young man only dreamed his adventure in the woods. Whether he did or not, his feelings about his fellowmen are permanently affected, although the others in the village go about their business as they did before. You will notice that he is called "Goodman Brown" several times in the last few paragraphs. He is no longer "Young Goodman" because he has been initiated into manhood now, despite the fact that he separates himself from other men and lives his life alone. Why? Just because of a single night's venture into the woods? Because of a pink ribbon? Because of a peculiar dream?

All you can do is put questions to yourself: What would *I* have done? Could I, having seen what Goodman thinks he saw, hold on to my faith?

The Minister's Black Veil, p. 32

THIS STORY begins on a sunny Sunday in the little New England town of Milford. If it were not for the title and that dark word *parable* beneath it, you might expect this to be a pleasant rural tale. Everything seems so simple and natural at first, with the children dressed in their best and the unmarried young men trying to flirt with the pretty girls. Then, suddenly, there is a breathless pause; and, when Parson Hooper appears, it is as if a cloud has blotted out the sun.

You may feel as troubled and surprised as the congregation — bustling, rustling, craning necks to see the amazing sight. (But why is that very old man so unperturbed, when some of the women are so upset they have to leave the meetinghouse?) Anyone would be shocked and mystified to see a familiar face unexpectedly draped in black cloth.

Parson Hooper *does* explain his reason when he gives his sermon; and, in some mysterious way, everybody understands. They all try to deny it later, of course, either by laughing very loud or by sinking into deep thought; and many of them try to think of some "sensible" reasons, although the doctor is sure "something must surely be amiss with Mr. Hooper's intellects." The important thing, though, on this first day of the veil's appearance, is that Mr. Hooper is left to walk — and have his Sunday dinner — all alone.

A funeral and a wedding take place on that same day, and, if you let yourself visualize the wedding candles and the bride's white face, you will not find it hard to believe in the possibility "that the maiden who had been buried a few hours before was come from her grave to be married." The black veil casts a pall on everything. Parson Hooper himself is horrified when he sees it in the mirror.

Why then does he keep it on? Why does he even refuse the simple request of Elizabeth, his "plighted wife," and permit a mere piece of cloth to deny him the happiness of marriage? Everyone in his village wonders and talks about it. A child trying to imitate him in fun only succeeds in terrifying his playmates and himself. Yet no one tries "to put the plain question to Mr. Hooper, wherefore he did this thing."

As Mr. Hooper explains to Elizabeth, the veil is "a type and a symbol." A symbol, of course, is something that stands for something else. Often, as in the case of Mr. Hooper's scrap of black crape, it is something material that stands for something immaterial: an idea, a feeling, an invisible state of things. The American flag is a material thing (also made of cloth), which — according to tradition and long-standing popular agreement — stands for the United States of America. The veil in this story, however, is an arbitrary symbol: Mr. Hooper, for his own reasons, deliberately chose to use it to represent something he himself had in mind. Like a symbol used in a work of literature (the forest, for instance, in "Young Goodman Brown" or the pink ribbon), it cannot be simply explained in response to a "plain question." Those who confront it may, by using their imaginations, discover within their own experience something which makes them recognize somehow what the symbol "means."

Parson Hooper realizes this. He believes that his piece of cloth will be recognized as something more than an emblem of his own sorrow or his own "secret sin." (The mention of Mr. Moody, at the beginning, may be meant to suggest that a veil on a minister's face need not mean one thing only. "In his case," writes Hawthorne, "the symbol had a different import.") In Parson Hooper's case, the import may remind you of Goodman Brown's discovery in the forest. And, although the Parson remains kind and loving, although he becomes remarkable enough to be called "Father Hooper," he too lives on "unloved, and dimly feared."

And so the "parable" works itself out; but the mystery which the story itself "obscurely typifies" is not the one the minister thinks it is. Something else has been expressed in this tale of old New England. It has to do with a value Nathaniel Hawthorne made basic to all of his work: the value of being a "brother-man."

Feathertop: A Moralized Legend, p. 53

WE HAVE BEEN WARNED before we begin this tale. It is a legend, Hawthorne tells us in his title, a story handed down over the generations, a story which may — or may not — be true. Because it is called "a *moralized* legend," whether it is true or not, we must take it seriously. We know that this is going to be more than a fairy story; the plight of Mother Rigby's scarecrow is intended to tell us something about the plight of man.

Finding yourself in Mother Rigby's cottage (with its invisible genie and its equally invisible hearth), you must try to see at least what can be seen. There is the glow of fire, as there so frequently is in Hawthorne's strangely lit scenes; and there is the duskiness of smoke. Notice how the narrator announces almost immediately that he cannot explain the source of the coal that lights Mother Rigby's pipe. He will admit to this inability to explain whenever the story takes a remarkable turn; and he will do so because he wants you to enter the game he is playing as he recounts his tale, and to play it according to his rules. You are to "suspend disbelief." You are asked to do that, to some degree, whenever you read a work of fiction; but here, in a realm of witches and scarecrows who come to life, you must make a special effort to believe what is happening.

The mood here is quite different at first from the mood prevailing in "Young Goodman Brown" and "The Minister's Black Veil." Mother Rigby is presented, without hesitation, as an expert witch, "the most cunning and potent in New England." She is full of invention, and she is alarmingly wise. Notice how ingenious she is when it comes to costuming her scarecrow with odds and ends left over from the historic past. Is it, do you think, an accident that the plum-colored coat was made in London and that the scarlet breeches were once worn "by the French governor of Louisbourg"? Or that all this "tattered finery" is to be worn by a creature whose head is nothing but a withered American pumpkin?

Suddenly, as you become more and more aware of glowing coal, puffs of smoke, and yellow face, you will probably be quite ready to accept the witch's pride in her creation. She begins talking like a mother, a particularly wise mother who is well acquainted with the world of men. Notice that she combines sustaining love with urging and goading: "Why lurkest thou in the corner, lazy one?" How many mothers do you know who are strong enough to dispatch their sons to face the world on their own? Feathertop finally moves off in the sunlight, walking "manfully" toward the town. He has learned to speak. If he had not, he would be helpless in society. He can say things like "Really!" and "Upon my word!"; and, because she has taught him to use the small change of social chit-chat, the witch insists he has a "pretty wit." She means that he is educated now, that he has learned the ways of the world.

Notice the glisten and shine of Feathertop's appearance, at least at the moments when he is puffing at his pipe. Why is it that he appears so brilliant and so dignified when the smoke is swirling about him, so "dim and faded" when his coal dies out? Can it be that the smoke gets in the spectators' eyes? And does not the little boy who screams something about a pumpkin remind you of the child in "The Emperor's New Clothes"?

The narrator, still playing his game, will not tell you what Feathertop whispers to Justice Gookin to frighten him so much. Nor will he fully explain why Polly (who is "neither very shrewd nor very simple") is so entranced with the courteous and well-behaved stranger. Even in our own day, girls are attracted to handsome fellows who know just how to dress and talk, who are, let us say, "cool." At some moments in history, gold-laced hats and velvet waistcoats insured success; at other moments, gray flannel suits might do the same; at still others, sandals and blue jeans.

A mirror breaks the spell. Mirrors, puddles, and fragments of glass are not uncommon in Hawthorne's work. (Remember the mirror in which Mr. Hooper sees himself in "The Minister's Black Veil" and how it terrifies him.) You may want to see the mirror as another symbol. It is true that a person can see himself, his physical self, in any mirror. But does he really see his true, his essential self? If he did, if anybody did, what would he see? Is the "outside show," for a human being, too, mere witchcraft?

The last scene, even with Mother Rigby's words about how Feathertop differs from the people who bustle selfishly around the "empty and heartless world," moves swiftly. There is neither radiance nor swirling smoke now, but only the rags and sticks of reality. Reality? You will wonder, along with the narrator. The story ends where it began, with the witch calling out for another coal. Without illusion, without "conventionalism" in speech and appearance, how would you know what was real?

Wakefield, p. 83

THIS IS ONE of the few stories Hawthorne wrote about places far from New England. It is based, as he says, on an actual event he had seen described in a newspaper or magazine; but, even so, it is one of his most personal stories. The experience presented seems very close — in tone, at least, and mood — to one the writer had lived through himself.

Hawthorne's mother became a recluse when her sea-captain husband died far away at sea; she lived for forty years without leaving her room in the Hawthorne house in Salem. His sisters, Elizabeth and Louisa, lived separately and silently in the same house; and Hawthorne spent more than ten years in seclusion there, seldom going out except at night to walk the streets under the moon. He knew very well how it felt to be out of sight. His neighbors, in fact, scarcely realized that he existed. And yet he had been very much in the world when he was a college student at Bowdoin. Hawthorne was certainly not an ordinary, sluggish, unimaginative man like the central character of this story; he spent most of his time learning the craft of writing when he was in retreat from the world. But it would seem that only a man who had made himself an outcast for some period in his life could become so preoccupied with as "remarkable a freak" as Wakefield.

This does not mean, of course, that this story is to be read as a piece of autobiography. In a sense every work of fiction is autobiographical, because writers (like all of us) must begin with their own experiences when they present their pictures of the world. Their experiences, however, are treated as raw material, to be transformed, molded, made into literary art. On occasion, the experiences selected for use are particularly unusual or particularly intimate; and this may be the case with "Wakefield." If you see it this way, you may be able to feel it as a kind of effort on Hawthorne's part to look at — and, in some measure, understand — what really happens when a person steps aside from "the system" and exposes himself to the strangeness of "our mysterious world."

The setting may surprise you because it will seem so modern and so recognizable. If you have never been to London, you probably have seen some English movies and are familiar with the misty, shabby look of some of the residential streets where the ordinary people live. You can easily visualize the dusky evening look of the shopping sections, with the crowds hurrying by and, more than likely, the rain falling on the umbrellas and abstracted faces. You can visualize the housefronts, too, with their stoops and their front windows. Behind those windows are, you know, the household firesides, the tea kettles, the humdrum routines of common life. Try to move with thin, unremarkable Wakefield through those streets and before those windows. Try, at the same time, to do what the narrator says: "Watch him long enough to see what we have described. . . ."

Would you say Wakefield is "mad"? Or is he too ordinary, too uninteresting, even when he finally recognizes "all the miserable strangeness of his life"? Try not to overlook the fact that he remains "in the bustle of the city," that he is "still involved in human interests," even though he is isolated and alone.

You may find yourself torn between two alternative explanations: on the one hand, what happens to Wakefield may seem perfectly possible in a big, indifferent city; on the other hand, what happens may seem utterly impossible — and absurd. Just as one Hawthorne story may be "natural" and "supernatural" at once, so another may be realistic and absurd at once. Does this say anything about the universe itself? Or about what it means to live hermitlike, to "cop out" for no good reason in the very midst of life?

The Ambitious Guest, p. 96

Ambitious is a word with many connotations: it may arouse a variety of feelings, summon up all kinds of associations. It is a word used to describe a man's proper desire to do his work and progress to the next stage. It is used to describe an impatient, somewhat improper desire to get ahead. It was used in classical literature to describe an excessive thirst for prominence or fame — or the "overreaching" which was punishable by the gods.

Ambition seems very remote from the contented family sitting around the fireplace at the beginning of this story. The firelight seems warm and comforting; it protects these people from the cold and the shrieking winds. Even so, you will feel a momentary chill when you realize the danger in that White

Mountain Notch, and the steepness of the mountain just above.

When you begin to read the story, you are back in New England with its rough-hewn grandeur, its cottage and tavern life. As you discover very soon, the day of the stern Puritan has passed. The day of trade and "internal commerce" has begun; there are roads through the mountains now, with stagecoaches, carts, and solitary wayfarers moving back and forth. It is probably the eighteenth century; people no longer spend their lives in confined communities, protected from the turbulent world. A man like the simple innkeeper in this story can think of being elected to the General Court, because "a plain, honest man may do as much good there as a lawyer." There is a restlessness in the wind; there is a spreading sense that anything is possible even for the plainest of men.

When the haunted-looking young traveler comes in, you will see how ready he is to forget differences in class and education. Reserved though he is, committed though he is to his lonely quest, he responds to the warmth he finds and pours out his heart to the "simple mountaineers," just as they do to him. Is that really because of their common fate? Or is it because, basically, they are all the same?

You can understand much better than could the readers in Hawthorne's time why a person should fear namelessness so much. If you have ever found yourself lost in a crowd, you know how terrible it is to feel unnoticed, unseen. Many young people think of growing up as a process of "making a name" for themselves. It is as if they are treated as mere statistics when they are young, mere abstractions ("teenagers," "adolescents," "youth"); and, like the traveler in Hawthorne's story, they cannot bear to think that, when they are old or dead, no one will even ask who they were. Not to be noticed is to feel as if one did not exist. Can you blame the guest for being ambitious? Or the father for thinking of "things that are pretty certain never to come to pass"?

Before long, though, you notice a considerable difference between the responses of the men and those of the women and children. The mother says they are in "a strange way, tonight"; the daughter feels suddenly lonely; the grandmother speaks of mirrors and death; the little boy demands a nighttime visit to the Flume. Perhaps because they are the ones who want security and contentment most of all, they find it hardest to "chase away the gloom." The dreary wailing of the wind keeps the children awake; the daughter has feelings which cannot be put into words.

What can you say about the ironic ending? The contest between fireside and mountain, which has gone on secretly throughout the story, is now over; and both, strangely enough, survive. The little mountain family will become a legend. But what of the guest? Did he bring obliteration on himself? You will want to sit very still for a moment when the tale is over. Is there an answer somewhere? Who knows?

The Wives of the Dead, p. 109

THIS STORY takes place, like "The Ambitious Guest," early in the eighteenth century. (Hawthorne makes this clear; he says it happened "a hundred years ago.") Again you are asked to visualize, since the setting is sketched in, as if for a painting or an actual stage set. Notice how domestic the picture is and how quickly you are made to realize that the "little curiosities" decorating the parlor are signs that one person is (or has been) at sea, and that another is (or has been) among the Indians. You are made aware, almost immediately, of the contrast between the "rainy twilight" of the New England seaport and that which lies beyond — in the dangerous forests of Canada and out on the stormy sea.

The image of the women left at home to weep will not be unfamiliar to you. Fishermen, sailors, and soldiers are forced to leave their wives in generation after generation; and often, too often, they never return. The unusual thing here is that the two lost husbands are brothers, and that the two widows live together, united once as sisters-in-law and now as "wives of the dead."

But the writer allows them just an hour of weeping before he presents them as two entirely different people. One of them is quiet, stoical, and practical; the other one is rebellious and desperate, finding it hard to resign herself, finding it difficult to sleep. You will find yourself sharing Margaret's sleeplessness for a time. Hawthorne will make you see with startling clarity the sitting room between the two bedrooms, the coldly flickering lamp, and the empty chairs. He will make you see, as if you too were peering out of the second-story window, the "lantern reddening the front of the house, and melting its light in the neighboring puddles. . . ." Again, you may be struck by the use this author makes of contrasts, particularly the contrast between firelight and darkness, between the gleam of a lantern and the "indistinct shapes of things."

You will see just as clearly the way the street looks after the rain, with the moon among the clouds, and the puddles turning silver on the rain-wet roofs. Then there will be the shadowed room again and the lamp shining down on a sleeping face. You will feel as if you too are tiptoeing between the rooms, opening and closing the latticed window, opening and closing doors.

But the last line will startle you and thrust you out again into a hazy, indistinct world. How can you bring the fragments together, "like order glimmering through chaos"? How can you tell what is real — whether one or both of the wives had a dream? After all, you were enabled to *see*, as if through your own waking eyes. Did you really see, or did you only think so? And how will you ever be sure?

The Birthmark, p. 119

THE FIGURE of the scientist, whether represented by an atomic physicist of world renown, a cool young technician in a space center, or an inscrutable, white-smocked person in a science fiction movie, is in the foreground of our world picture today. Because science has become so complex and so specialized, because scientists generally speak a language unfamiliar to the layman, there is an aura of strangeness about them. When we think of the power locked up in their test tubes or made visible on their slides, we sometimes shrink a little. There is something almost magical about what they can do. Is it surprising that they remind us of that ancient magician named Merlin or other practitioners of what once were described as the "Black Arts"?

Aylmer, in this story, will strike you as strangely familiar, even though he lives just after electricity was discovered. If you think of his name as an anagram and scramble the letters a little, you will come up with something reminiscent of, although not identical with, "Merlin." But he is a relatively modern man, with a tremendous faith in the power of scientific thinking. He is the kind of man who would not be surprised at the news that we are now exploring outer space and contemplating sending men to the moon.

He is preoccupied, however, not with the moon, but with a tiny flaw on his wife's lovely face. The mark seems to him to be a sign not only of physical imperfection but of human frailty. The birthmark affects him as if it were a symbol of Georgiana's "liability to sin, sorrow, decay, and death." After all, the reader thinks, she is a human being, not a piece of statuary. Can it be that Aylmer is troubled by precisely those qualities which distinguish men and women from inanimate objects — and from gods and goddesses as well? And, when he devises his peculiar plan, is he not trying to use his scientific knowledge to conquer Nature herself?

The desire to discover Nature's fundamental secrets is probably as old as man himself; and there are many instances in literature of Nature fighting back when an individual explorer goes too far. You may remember the story of Faust who sold his soul for the sake of learning all there was to learn. You may know the story of Captain Ahab in *Moby Dick,* the "kinglike man" who destroyed himself and almost his entire crew in his mad pursuit of the white whale. You may have read Ernest Hemingway's *The Old Man and the Sea*, in which Santiago's "really big fish" is eaten, finally, by sharks.

In "The Birthmark," too, a man goes too far. Before you discover how far, you once again enter a world where everything that happens might actually happen in ordinary life. But then, again, there may be supernatural forces at work, expressing themselves in the symbol of the tiny hand, in the "smoky aspect" of Aylmer's half-human assistant, Aminadab, and even in the "enchantment" of the gorgeously draped rooms which once were the dingy laboratory. (Georgiana herself thinks those rooms might be "a pavilion among the clouds.") And surely the evocation of the alchemists' long search for the "elixir vitae," the secret liquid which would transform lead into gold, summons up a whole universe of magic and strange powers working in the earth.

The earth triumphs, of course. We still live in what Hawthorne calls a "sphere of half development." It is good to strive, to use one's capacities, to search. But you will tell yourself at the end that human beings must never try to achieve perfection or final answers to their questions — not if they want to stay human and retain their ability to love. Aylmer believes that he loves his wife more intensely the more he feels shocked by her imperfection; but his absorption in his experiment separates him wholly from her. See how he lashes out at her when she comes into his laboratory to tell him of her strange new symptom — and how he makes it impossible for her to tell. See, too, how Georgiana's faith in him, her blind exultation in his "honorable love," becomes a counterpoint to his blind manipulations — and destroys them both. No wonder the "man of clay" laughs!

Roger Malvin's Burial, p. 145

HAWTHORNE INTRODUCES YOU to the imaginary world of Roger Malvin and Reuben Bourne with a paragraph of confidences about the tricks of his trade. He says quite honestly that, although he is beginning with an actual incident in the Indian wars, his imagination is going to play with it — and that imagination works "by casting certain circumstances judicially in the shade." Also, he suggests that, although history must deal with masses of men, fiction concentrates on the "deeds of one or two individuals," deeds which may be just as renowned as those of entire armies. But there is something faintly ironic in what he says partly because "Lovell's Fight," which is his starting point, resulted in the death of most of those who took part. (And both sides were equally chivalrous, he writes.) In spite of the fatalities, Hawthorne tells you, the battle is considered important because it "broke the strength of a tribe" and led to some years of peace. Is he saying that the end justifies the means? Or that the death of some men is warranted if it helps others live their lives in peace?

Before you determine precisely what he means, you find yourself brought face to face with another of Hawthorne's carefully designed scenes. You see the sunlit treetops in the forest, the bed of leaves, the great veined rock of the hill, and two wounded men. And you find yourself, almost without preparation, caught up in the peculiar disagreement between the old man and young Reuben Bourne.

It is the kind of disagreement in which both participants are right; and this makes it strangely difficult for the reader to take sides. If you are finally convinced, as Reuben seems to have been by Roger Malvin's unselfish reasoning, you must consider the degree to which Reuben's choice "was aided, unconsciously to himself, by the hidden strength of many another motive." Have you ever been in a situation which demanded a fair and impartial decision of some kind — only to find yourself deciding to do what you wanted to do all the time? Have you ever found your own wishes coloring the "facts" you have tried to take into account, as Reuben's wishes did when they "seized on the thought that Malvin's life might be preserved"? No human being can be entirely rational and entirely objective when it comes to making choices, especially those choices which immediately affect his life. There are many hidden motives governing human behavior, no matter how sensible and unselfish an individual thinks he is.

Surely you can understand Reuben Bourne, even as you hope you will never have to make a decision

like the one he is forced to make. It may be harder
to accept the lie he tells to Dorcas. Could *you* admit,
though, that your "selfish love of life" made you do
what Reuben did? Pay heed to all Reuben's good
excuses by this time: he is recovering from his wound;
he has been unconscious for some days; he loves
Dorcas and wants to marry her. Ask yourself, "If I
were Reuben, what would I do?" (The answer should
remain your own secret.)

You will find Reuben rationalizing repeatedly —
finding good reasons for what he believes in any case;
but you will also find that "concealment had imparted to a justifiable act much of the secret effect
of guilt." He is caught, as people so often are, in the
consequences of his lie. He feels a compulsion to keep
the last promise he made to Roger Malvin, but he
denies it; and he becomes as sad and isolated as
Goodman Brown after his journey to the woods. For
Hawthorne, a secret guilt inevitably destroys a man,
as if it were "a serpent gnawing into his heart." A
poor farmer to begin with, Reuben becomes so
touchy he antagonizes people; and, although other
farmers are prosperous, his fortune rapidly declines.
He eventually does what many unsuccessful farmers
did in the eighteenth century: he makes up his mind
to take his wife and son and move westward toward
the frontier.

For Reuben, this means moving into the wilderness; and by now you know the ambiguities Hawthorne associates with the "deep recess of the forest."
You have only to think back to "Young Goodman
Brown." You may be startled, however, to find the
remarkable son of Reuben and Dorcas introduced
immediately after the mention of the forest. There is
something somehow excessive about the description
of young Cyrus: words like "beautiful" and "glorious"
are used; he is recognized as "a future leader," even

though he is only fifteen. Don't the phrases "His foot was fleet, his aim true, his apprehension quick, his heart glad and high" make you think of a youthful Greek hero, or perhaps a god? Isn't there something troubling about the presentation of such a vision after the talk of Reuben's "irritability," his "evil fate"?

Your unease may be heightened by the paragraph about the fantasied wilderness, the wishful wilderness, which is so remote from the one perceived by Reuben. The forest, of course, means one thing to Dorcas and Cyrus, quite another to the man with the "cold, cold sorrow" inside. You will be reminded again that we see what our inner selves permit us to see, just as we do what we secretly wish to do.

Does this explain what happens to the Bourne family on the twelfth of May? You will find that Dorcas's mention of the date confuses Reuben for a moment and then makes him say something that shows he has had one idea in mind all the time. Dorcas, quite naturally, talks of "my poor father." Can it be that Reuben, now a father himself, has thought of Roger Malvin as his own father — to whom he broke the most important promise he could have made?

You will think the ending of this story mysterious and horrifying unless you attend carefully to such words as "sleepwalker," "the strange influence," "the secret place of his soul where his motives lay hidden." It is in the end as it was in the beginning. Reuben Bourne does what he had to do, this time to expiate the guilt for a broken vow. The language and the imagery at the end may remind you of the Bible: there are tears "like water from a rock"; Reuben has "come to redeem" and, for the first time, utters a prayer.

But did he really sin? Was there really something to expiate? Or was it all in his mind, in some "secret place of his soul"?

My Kinsman, Major Molineux, p. 175

THERE IS A MOMENT in every young person's life when he must leave his home and family and go out into an alien world. There was a moment in American history when the colonists in New England began to stir restlessly under British rule and strike out, almost childishly at first, against its representatives. In this story, the moments coincide. Robin begins his search for his kinsman just when the people in Boston are becoming conscious of themselves as citizens with the right to govern themselves.

Massachusetts Bay Colony, as we have seen, had once been governed by the Puritan elders and magistrates who had secured a charter from the English King to create their New Jerusalem in the New World. That meant that they were entitled to establish the kind of government they chose; and they chose, of course, to build the theocratic, authoritarian state which led to such responses as Goodman Brown's and Parson Hooper's. In 1684, however, the Puritans lost their charter; and, although they remained in control in many villages, Massachusetts Bay became a royal colony. King James II, in order to manage it more effectively, made it part of the Dominion of New England, along with New York and New Jersey, under Governor Edmund Andros. In 1688, when King James was deposed by Parliament, the colonists rebelled, and the Dominion was dissolved. Although Connecticut and Rhode Island were permitted to return to self-government, Massachusetts was not; and, as Hawthorne writes at the beginning of this story, the governors continued to be appointed by the Crown.

By the time young Robin arrives in Boston, the discontents of the citizens have been accumulating for many decades. But Robin has grown up in the country and has never been to the city before. In the days before mass communications, people did not live in a single "village" as they do in the television age. Those who lived out in the country were very likely to be unaware of what was happening even thirty miles away. Robin's father, in any case, was a clergyman who had reared his children firmly, but in an innocent, sunlit world. How was he to imagine what impended for the impressive-looking gentleman who had visited him the previous year? Major Molineux was his cousin, after all; and, when he offered to give one of the clergyman's sons a start in life, no one was likely to doubt his word.

All this is background to the story, or its realistic frame. Once you see Robin crossing the ferry in the moonlight, you find yourself losing touch with what is merely factual, what is reliable and everyday. The only thing to do is to try to *become* Robin and see what happens through his wondering eyes. If it is his dream, try — at least for a moment — to make it yours as well.

You yourself may once have traveled to a strange city; and you too may even have arrived at night. If so, you can easily understand how Robin feels when he finds himself in the narrow, winding streets of Boston where he has never been before. Boston may have been a little town in those days, compared with what it is today; but you will be told that it is as fascinating to young Robin as if it were "London city." The darkness is bewildering; the people he meets are even more bewildering. But, at least at the beginning, it helps to know that his kinsman is an important man. Some day, the boy can tell himself, these peculiar people will know who he really is.

The feeling of groping and searching in an unfamiliar place is heightened by the emphasis on moonlit darkness ad mysterious half-light. Again, it is as if you were coming upon a sequence of theatrical

tableaux, swift little scenes interspersed with blank-
ness, as if projected by the old stereopticon once
known as the "Magic Box" — or, if you prefer, as if
caught by a mobile television camera trundled
through the winding alleys of the town. The poet,
Robert Lowell, made the story into a play not long
ago. When it was presented on a stage, the lights
were kept very dim, except when Robin had one of
his confrontations with the citizens of Boston. Then
one section of the stage would suddenly light up,
momentarily disclosing a barber shop, a tavern, or
shop windows.

Each character in the story is first seen indistinctly
in the distance and then becomes sharply visible as
Robin draws near, and a light from the window of
a house or a shop illuminates a periwig, a coat, a
skirt, a flushed and blackened face. You will feel
Robin's growing awareness of the annoyance, scorn,
and hostility which greet his innocent question:
"Whereabouts is the dwelling of my kinsman, Major
Molineux?" You will share his increasing perplexity,
until you too will be unable to think of a reasonable
explanation for the lack of respect shown by everyone he meets — he, the kinsman of Major Molineux.

And you will go on searching with him among the
unfamiliar faces and the nameless streets. He has to
cope (as we all do) with the unheeding crowds of
people in the shops and on the cobblestones: the
rough, hard-drinking sailors, the professionally smiling innkeeper, the elegant strollers who make him
feel embarrassed about his "natural, quiet gait." And
there is (as in the life of every youth) a girl, "a dainty
little figure, with a white neck, round arms, and a
slender waist." She wears a scarlet skirt and lives on
a shabby, waterfront street; but he is "half-willing"
to follow her across her threshold. He is stopped by
a "guardian of midnight order," a version of whom

has appeared in the course of everyone's growing up.

Then there are the men who appear and reappear: the old man with his sepulchral voice, muttering "authority," and the grotesque gentleman with the fiery eyes and the "double prominence" on his forehead, whose face changes until it seems to be red on one side, black on the other. (Is not Robin's whole vision of the moonlit town a vision of scarlet clashing with the night?) Finally, there is the kindly person who waits with Robin to see the major pass — and who tells him, at the end, that he can make his way in the world on his own.

You will have experienced by then a boy's coming to maturity, and you will wonder how and why. Is it because he lived through the puzzling night in that moonlit, alien town? Is it because he came at last to understand that, lonely as he felt, he had outgrown his sheltered life at home? Or is it because he was able to join the very citizens who had laughed at him in laughing at the spectacle of the marching mob "in frenzied merriment, trampling all on an old man's heart"?

You may have the same feeling Robin has at the end: a "feeling of ambiguity and weariness." You know that, less than half a century later, the "senseless uproar" of the citizens became a war for independence. You may wonder if young people, too, are required to reject and defy their kinsmen — and even to rebel against them — in order to establish their independence as individuals, to demonstrate that they are "shrewd" enough to be themselves.

Nathaniel Hawthorne—
A Biographical Sketch

NATHANIEL HAWTHORNE was a New Englander, born in Salem, Massachusetts in 1802. His father was a sea captain who died of yellow fever in the Far East when the boy was only four. His mother took to her room when his father died; his two sisters, Elizabeth and Louisa, were quiet, solitary girls. From his early childhood, he was acquainted with shadows and loneliness. It is not hard to understand why he was so caught up in his own imaginings and why he developed (as he said later) a "peephole" vision of the world.

He went to Bowdoin College and did make friends there. When he graduated in 1825, he returned to Salem; and, for almost twelve years, he spent most of his time hidden away in his room. He would go out in the evenings for lonely walks in the moonlight.

He would stand for hours sometimes, staring at a particular scene, looking at the lights and shadows, studying the way the component parts meshed into a whole.

He was learning his trade, you see, in those long, silent years. He made himself an apprentice in the craft of writing; and he seems to have believed that it was necessary to remain alone if he was to shape his own style and learn how to put his vision of life into words. In the summers he took trips around New England and once went west to Detroit. His trips were like field trips, during which he collected impressions of the people he met in inns and taverns or on stagecoaches. He kept a journal, and he jotted down all kinds of things as he traveled: little descriptions of the countryside; comments on individuals who caught his attention; whimsical ideas that later became the kernels of short stories. This is probably how he learned to create such compelling images of people and places. You can imagine him moving down the roads, catching brief glimpses of strange happenings among people he did not know — and then making a great effort to put what he felt and saw into words. Reading the stories, you will often feel the strangeness of what he saw. The feeling will be much like the one you have when you look by chance into a lighted window and see two people talking to each other, reading, or eating their dinner. It will be like the feeling you get when you pass through an unfamiliar city in a train. Things that seem normal if you or your friends are doing them take on a misty, unreal quality when seen from outside (or through a "peephole").

Hawthorne labored over his vision of the world, it happens, at a time when the people around him were mostly engaged in doing very different things. Salem was a bustling seaport at that period. The streets and shops and warehouses were alive with all sorts of busy, ambitious merchants and seamen. You may remember that Andrew Jackson was elected President of the United States in 1828, and that his terms in office are frequently called the time of emergence for "the common man." Not only were the businessmen busily working to get rich and powerful, mechanics and artisans everywhere were using their votes and demanding their rights. They, too, wanted to be independent, to get ahead. Sometimes, when there were not enough jobs, there were riots and street demonstrations. People wanted security and comfort; they wanted, perhaps more than anything else, material success.

Picture Nathaniel Hawthorne, then, living his odd, impractical life in the center of a boisterous, materialistic society. He could not have been more of an outsider; and it is no wonder that so few people even knew he was alive. It is always hard to be a practicing artist in a middle-class, sensible world. It is especially hard when you are — or feel yourself to be — alone. If Hawthorne had lived in Boston, he might have found himself a group of fellow artists and lived a kind of bohemian life. The fact that he did not must certainly have intensified his understanding of separateness and, at the same time, his understanding of how important it was to make connections, to be "a brother-man."

He wrote one novel, named *Fanshawe,* when he was in seclusion and paid to have it published anonymously. A little later, the Salem *Gazette* printed some of his stories. Then, perhaps after he felt he had finished his apprenticeship, he managed to tear himself away from his "owl's nest" and went to Boston to edit a magazine, but his salary was never paid.

In 1837, he published some of the stories he had been writing in a collection called *Twice-Told Tales.*

The poet, Henry Wadsworth Longfellow, who had been in Hawthorne's class at Bowdoin, praised the stories in print. Obviously, this was a good year for Hawthorne. He met beautiful fragile Sophia Peabody at that time, after her older sister, Elizabeth, had decided he should come to the Peabody house for a visit. Elizabeth Peabody was one of the best known female intellectuals of her day. Teacher, writer, reformer, she taught school with Bronson Alcott, started the first kindergarten in New England, and became involved in every sort of humanitarian crusade. Her sister, Maria, later married Horace Mann, the great pioneer of public education. Sophia, whom she thought too frail to marry anyone, became Hawthorne's "belovedest"; and they were engaged the year after they met.

His love for Sophia did a great deal to move him into "the midst of life." You can see in many of his stories his realization of the importance of relationships like the one he had with Sophia. Those relationships, he often seemed to suggest, are what keep a man from becoming a kind of monster. They tie him to the rest of humanity and keep him from becoming stern and cold, as Goodman Brown did after his visit to the woods, or as Reuben Bourne did.

His plan to marry Sophia gave him a very practical reason for making money. He sought and was given a political appointment to the Salem Customs House, the very place where he claimed to have found the scrap of red cloth which suggested his novel, *The Scarlet Letter*. Many leading intellectuals and artists at that time were interested in a new Utopian community that had opened at Brook Farm; and, in 1841, Hawthorne decided to give the community a try. He knew he would need a home for himself and Sophia; and, for a while, he thought it would be rewarding to live the simple, communal life with other people who were interested in art and in ideas. He did not stay very long, however, because he could not endure it. He realized that human beings are simply too imperfect (too human, perhaps) to live together in a perfectly peaceful and productive community. You can find this skepticism about human perfection in stories like "Young Goodman Brown" and "The Birthmark." Hawthorne seems to have thought it to be a kind of aberration for anyone to expect perfection or utopia. Later on, he presented his vision of Brook Farm in a novel called *The Blithedale Romance*, published in 1852.

He married his Sophia the year after he left Brook Farm and was lucky enough to be given Emerson's house, the Old Manse, in Concord, the town where Emerson and Thoreau both lived. Not far from the town were the woods and Walden Pond made famous by Thoreau. You may be able to see a connection between the nearness of those woods and Hawthorne's preoccupation with the wilderness in his tales of New England in an earlier day. Eventually he left Concord and went back to work at the Salem Customs House. He then published the stories he had written in Concord and called them *Mosses from an Old Manse*.

Hawthorne was a Democrat; and, when the Whigs took over the government in 1848, he lost his job at the Customs House. This was a good thing, as it turned out, because he was about ready to do some of his best writing. In 1850, the very year after he left Salem, he published *The Scarlet Letter*. Then he moved to a farmhouse in the Berkshire Mountains, near Lenox, Massachusetts. (The farmhouse is still there, right near the entrance to the Tanglewood Music Festival grounds.) In 1851 he published *House of the Seven Gables*.

When he was in the Berkshires, he met Herman

Melville, who was in the process of writing *Moby Dick*. The two artists became good friends during the single summer they spent together; and it is often said that it was Hawthorne, with his interest in symbols and figurative language, who influenced Melville to transform a book that started out as a simple story about whaling into that poetic, mysterious novel entitled *Moby Dick*.

Soon after, Hawthorne and his family moved back to Concord, where they bought a house. It may seem odd; but, in 1852, while living in Concord, he wrote the campaign biography for Franklin Pierce, his old friend and classmate, who went on to be elected President. Because of his association with Pierce, Hawthorne was appointed United States Consul at Liverpool in England and had a chance to see some of the countries in Europe, which struck him as far more romantic and far more conducive to romantic writing than the practical, success-haunted environment at home. He went to Italy, where he wrote his last novel, *The Marble Faun*, and where his little daughter became so sick she almost died. He loved the little girl and probably understood her very well. His affection for and knowledge of children, in fact, are visible in many of his stories. Think of that little boy in "Feathertop," the impish child in "The Minister's Black Veil," the one who wants to visit the Flume in "The Ambitious Guest." Or, if you like, think of the adolescents in the stories: Cyrus, for example, and Robin. Surely Hawthorne knew of what he spoke.

Ill himself, he came back to Concord in 1860 and found it very difficult to work on his writing. About all he could do was a collection of sketches about England, which he dedicated to Franklin Pierce, who had by then lost all his popularity. Then, in 1864, while on a trip with Pierce, Hawthorne died in his sleep in Plymouth, New Hampshire.

His life, as you see, was varied. It seems to have been broken up, almost as his stories are, into separate, dimly lit scenes. No one was better able to transform his own experiences with places and human beings into art. No one was more gifted when it came to working with words. And, perhaps most significantly of all, no one was more familiar with what Melville was to call (in a review of Hawthorne's work) "the power of blackness," the mystery and darkness at the heart of life. Only when a man can perceive that darkness can he help others to appreciate the light.

**A SELECTIVE BIBLIOGRAPHY
OF NATHANIEL HAWTHORNE**

WORKS BY NATHANIEL HAWTHORNE

The Complete Novels and Selected Tales of Nathaniel Hawthorne, edited by Norman H. Pearson. Modern Library, a division of Random House, Inc.

* *The Portable Hawthorne,* edited by Malcolm Cowley. Viking Press Inc.

* *The Blithedale Romance.*

* *House of the Seven Gables* (Scholastic Book Services T 640).

* *The Marble Faun.*

* *The Scarlet Letter* (Scholastic Book Services T 320).

Titles marked with an asterisk (°) are available in paperback.

BIOGRAPHY AND CRITICISM

Brooks, Van Wyck. *The Flowering of New England.* New York: E. P. Dutton.

* Howard, Leon. *Literature and the American Tradition.* New York: Anchor Books, Doubleday.

* Levin, Harry. *The Power of Blackness: Hawthorne, Poe, Melville.* Vintage Books, Alfred A. Knopf, 1958.

Marx, Leo. *The Machine in the Garden: Technology and the Pastoral Ideal in America.* New York: Oxford University Press, 1964.

Matthiessen, F. O. *American Renaissance.* New York: Oxford University Press, 1941.

* Starkey, Marion L. *The Devil in Massachusetts.* New York: Dolphin Books, Doubleday.

Stewart, Randall. *Nathaniel Hawthorne.* New Haven, Conn.: Yale University Press, 1948.

Van Doren, Mark, *Nathaniel Hawthorne, a Critical Biography.* New York: Viking Press, 1957.

Wagenknecht, Edward C. *Nathaniel Hawthorne.* New York: Oxford University Press, 1961.

Waggoner, Hyatt H. *Hawthorne: A Critical Study.* Cambridge, Mass.: Harvard University Press, revised edition, 1963.

* Wolfe, Don M., *The Image of Man in America.* New York: McGraw-Hill Book Company, 1957.